PICTURES
IN THE DARK

PICTURES
IN THE DARK

GILLIAN CROSS

HOLIDAY HOUSE / NEW YORK

Copyright © Gillian Cross 1996
First published 1996 by Oxford University Press
in Great Britain

Library of Congress Cataloging-in-Publication Data
Cross, Gillian.
Pictures in the dark / Gillian Cross.
p.   cm.
Summary: A chance photograph taken for the school Camera Club
draws Charlie into the emotionally troubled lives of his classmate
Jennifer's family, especially that of her younger brother who
harbors an astounding secret.
ISBN 0-8234-1267-9 (alk. paper)
[1. Photography—Fiction.   2. Emotional problems—Fiction.
3. Prejudices—Fiction.   4. Human-animal relationships—Fiction.
5. Otters—Fiction.   6. England—Fiction.]   I. Title.
PZ7.C88253Pi   1996   96-7660   CIP   AC
[Fic]—dc20

PICTURES
IN THE DARK

Chapter One

It was on the last day of August that Charlie Willcox took the strangest photograph of his life.

Black and orange.

He'd spent the whole evening adding to his collection of funny family pictures. Catching Alison and Bill, his aunt and uncle, covered in smuts from the barbecue. Snapping his cousins, Zoë and Rachel, with their mouths full of sausage. Getting a wonderful shot of his mother, with a French loaf balanced on her head. Now it was midnight, and all he wanted was his bed.

He only stopped on the Old Bridge to give his parents a chance to catch up. Because he was tired, he leaned on the parapet, gazing down at the water, and that was when he saw it.

Black and orange.

The wide smooth surface of the river was completely black, except for a pool of orange light from the street lamp behind him. His own head and shoulders, jutting above the parapet, made a stark, black silhouette in the middle of the orange pool.

He had both his cameras with him, and there was one shot left on the film in the Minolta. When he saw the pattern of black and orange, he suddenly thought, *Why not have a go?* Mr Feinstein was always nagging on in the Camera Club about taking more adventurous pictures.

Charlie took a step to the right, so that his silhouette was exactly in the middle of the patch of orange. He rested his elbows on the parapet and paused, with his finger on the button, just to check that the camera didn't show.

And, in that instant, the picture shattered.

Something struck across the pool of light, swimming fast. The smooth orange surface was fractured by a strong, V-shaped pattern of ripples and Charlie's silhouette cracked into jazzy, irregular stripes. *Drat!* he thought.

It was too late to stop his finger. It was already pressing the shutter release, to take the photograph.

'But what *is* it?' Mr Feinstein held the print high, so that everyone in the Camera Club could see.

'It's the river,' Charlie said stoutly.

'Black? And orange? With all those lines?' Mr Feinstein raised a sarcastic eyebrow.

Charlie wasn't going to back off. 'That's how it looked. The orange was coming from a street lamp, and something swam through the light. You can see the wake.'

Mr Feinstein made a big show of inspecting the picture again. 'Some wake. What was it? A hippo?'

Everyone laughed.

'No, sir—a dolphin!'

'A blue whale!'

'A nuclear submarine!'

Whatever had made the ripples was just beyond the light. The point of the V was chopped off, drawing attention to the darkness at the edges of the picture. Leaving people free to imagine monsters.

Mr Feinstein let them fantasize for a minute. Then he grinned, deflatingly. 'It was a dog. Wasn't it, Charlie?'

Charlie was sure it hadn't been a dog. But he wasn't going to argue, because he'd thought of a brilliant answer. 'Who cares what it was?' he said loftily. 'That picture isn't natural history. It's Art!'

That was just the sort of thing Mr Feinstein was always saying to them. Charlie got a laugh and a round of applause, and Mr Feinstein grinned and waved the print at him.

'OK, Leonardo, I give in. Whatever it is, it's a great image. Can I put it in the Jolly Holiday Snaps display?'

Charlie tried not to look as pleased as he felt. Mr Feinstein was very choosy about what went into the Camera Club displays. Not many Year Nines got a photograph on the board.

'If you like,' he said casually.

'I do like.' Mr Feinstein laid the picture down and shuffled a hand through the rest of the prints on the table. 'It'll liven up this load of junk. I've never seen so many Beautiful Views and Famous Sights. You're all getting picture postcard minds.'

He picked up one or two other photographs, pulled a face, and scooped the whole lot together.

'I'll choose the rest of the display tonight. You can put it up, Willcox.' He nodded at Charlie. 'Come in and do it tomorrow lunch time. And you'll need someone to help.' He glanced round the room. 'How about you, Jennifer? Meet me by the display board at twelve thirty.'

He didn't wait for an answer. He just slid the photographs into a folder and strode out of the room. Charlie turned and looked over his shoulder. Since when had Jennifer Luttrell started coming to the Camera Club? She'd been in his tutor group for three years, and he'd never heard her mention photography.

There she was though, shrinking into a corner at the back. Neat school uniform. Mousy pony-tail. Inconspicuous as usual. Charlie called across to her.

'Can you make it tomorrow, then? To do the display?'

Jennifer shrugged and picked up her bag. 'If I skip choir.'

'No need for that.' Charlie didn't particularly fancy spending a whole lunch hour with her, racking his brains for things to say. 'I can tell Mr Feinstein where you are.'

'No, I'll come,' Jennifer said stiffly. She came down the room and opened the door, holding it for Charlie to go through. 'I want to talk to him anyway. I need some advice about cameras.'

'He'll give you stacks of advice.' Charlie grinned as they walked down the corridor. 'What kind of camera have you got now?'

'I haven't. I just want—' Jennifer went suddenly and startlingly pink. 'I'm just beginning.'

Charlie couldn't remember anyone else who'd joined the Camera Club without even a camera. He gave her a curious glance. 'What sparked that off, then?'

'Nothing,' Jennifer muttered. *And mind your own business*, said her voice. She turned her head away, looking down at the floor.

Great, thought Charlie. She said something faintly interesting and when you tried to talk about it, you ran smack into a brick wall. They were going to have a scintillating time putting up the display. He opened the door out to the field.

'See you later, then.'

He was just about to streak off and find Keith, when he noticed the gaggle of new kids streaming across the field. They were heading for the far side, where a little crowd had already gathered, by the wall.

'What's going on?' Jennifer said sharply.

'Dunno. Probably a fight.' Charlie wasn't really interested. There was always some kind of row in the lunch hour. He

4

wouldn't have given it a second thought, except for the wail that came suddenly from the middle of the crowd.

It was shrill and tearful. Charlie couldn't make out the words, but he recognized the voice all right, even from the other side of the field. It was his cousin Rachel.

Poor old Raz. She'd only been there a week, and she wasn't tough like Zoë. He'd better go and make sure she was all right. He set off across the field, forgetting all about Jennifer.

He was ready to elbow his way through the crowd, but he didn't need to. As soon as he arrived, people turned round, all itching to tell someone what had happened.

'He made her fall off the wall!'

'He made her!'

'Look. She's hurt her knee.'

'She's bleeding!'

Ghoulish little monsters. They were really enjoying themselves. Charlie raised his voice and bellowed above the noise. 'How can I hear if you all talk at once? Who's bleeding?'

It was Rachel. She was standing in the middle of the crowd, looking pale and shaky. Blood was trickling down her sock from a great gash on one knee. And next to her was Zoë, square and solid, with an arm round her shoulders. Playing the heroic elder sister.

'What's happened?' Charlie said.

Zoë pointed at Rachel's knee, as though he might not have noticed it. 'Look!'

Charlie looked. Then he looked up at the wall. It was two metres high and strictly out of bounds, but the Year Sevens always had a go at walking along it. And they quite often fell off.

'So?' he said.

Rachel looked down at the ground, scuffing the dust with one foot, but Zoë's eyes flamed.

'So? Is that all you can say? Rachel was on the highest bit of the wall. The very highest bit. And *he*—' She whisked round suddenly and grabbed at someone behind her. 'He made her fall. What are you going to do about it?'

That was typical. Zoë was always leaping into arguments and expecting Charlie to back her up, because he was a year older.

'Hang on a minute,' Charlie said. He looked at the boy she'd dragged out of the crowd. He was obviously new, like Rachel. Small and skinny, with hair cropped short and ears that stuck out. His school uniform hung round him in baggy folds. 'What happened?'

The boy stared down at the ground. 'Don't know,' he muttered.

Charlie sighed and turned to Rachel. 'Well? What did he do? Did he pull your feet?'

Rachel shook her head.

'Shout at you?'

Another shake.

'Oh, come *on*. Did he tell you a joke that was so funny that you fell off the wall laughing?'

'It's nothing,' Rachel said gruffly. 'All right? It doesn't matter.'

Lowering her head, she pushed past Charlie and wriggled through the crowd. Zoë let go of the boy's shoulder, with a quick, impatient snort.

'I'll go after her. *Someone* ought to make sure she washes that knee.'

She glared reproachfully at Charlie and shoved past him, following Rachel. Everyone else began to sidle away. Whispering and glancing back at Charlie.

He had a curious feeling that they all knew something that he didn't. Something unsettling. But no one told him what it was. He was left facing the boy who had caused all the fuss.

He didn't look like a trouble-maker. He was small and bony and he stood very still, with his head hanging down. Only his fingers moved, picking restlessly at the bottom of his sweatshirt.

'What *did* you do?' Charlie said.

'Didn't do anything,' the boy mumbled, hardly loud enough to be heard.

'Don't give me that. I'm not saying you made her fall off the wall, but you must have done something.'

The boy raised his head and gave Charlie a long, stubborn stare. 'I didn't do anything.'

His eyes were very pale, like water over pebbles, and Charlie had the most extraordinary urge to grab him by the shoulders and shake, as hard as he could. Shake and shake, until the strange, obstinate look was wiped off his face.

Instead, he clenched his fists and pushed them into his pockets. 'Well, whatever it was, you'd better not do it again. See?'

'I didn't do anything,' the boy said, more loudly this time.

Then he bolted, scuttling past Charlie and running across the field with short, awkward strides. Charlie spun round and realized, for the first time, that the two of them hadn't been alone. Jennifer Luttrell was standing right behind him.

He laughed, awkwardly, as if she'd caught him at a disadvantage. 'What a weird boy. Did you see his eyes? If he looked at Rachel like that, I'm not surprised she fell off the wall.'

He meant to sound casual and amused, but he was more shaken than he had realized, and the words came out jerkily.

Jennifer didn't react at all. She stared past him, frowning at the skinny boy who was running away from them.

'Oh well,' Charlie said. 'I expect he'll settle in, in a week or two. He's in for a tough time if he doesn't.'

Scanning the field, he saw Keith waving at him from the far side. Thankfully he seized the excuse and escaped to play football.

It was only much later that he realized how oddly Jennifer had behaved. She hadn't said a single word.

Chapter Two

She was still silent when they met at lunch time next day, to put up the Jolly Holiday Snaps. Charlie made a few attempts to start a conversation while they were waiting for Mr Feinstein, but all he could get out of her was *Yes* and *No*. In the end, he gave up and lounged round the foyer, peering at Year Ten's life drawings.

'No time for art appreciation,' Mr Feinstein said, annoyingly, when he arrived ten minutes late. 'There's work to do.' He planted himself in an armchair and sent a handful of prints slithering across the coffee table. 'Right then. How are you going to arrange these?'

Charlie hadn't expected a question like that. He looked down at the pictures. Most of them were fairly ordinary holiday photographs—beaches and castles, and swimming pools in Florida. But there was a sprinkling of odd ones, like his black and orange river.

'We could sort them into different subjects,' he said.

Mr Feinstein groaned, loudly and dramatically. 'Willcox, you have the artistic sense of a flea! This is an exhibition, not a filing system. We want an arrangement to draw the pictures together. To make a statement. For instance . . . '

He leaned forward, spreading the prints with one hand. Behind his back, Charlie pulled a face at Jennifer. *Here we go. Another wonderful D. Feinstein scheme.* But she didn't respond.

'We'll put this in the centre.' Mr Feinstein pulled Charlie's photograph out of the heap and laid it on one side. 'Then we'll have the other odd ones radiating out from that. The conventional ones can fill in the gaps, and that'll give us a web of strangeness against an ordinary background.'

He looked up suddenly, catching Charlie off guard, and his snort was almost amused.

'What's the matter? Don't you think it'll work?'

'Why does there have to be a plan?' Charlie said rebelliously. 'They're all separate pictures, taken by different people. Why can't we just put them up as they come, without making a fuss?'

Jennifer looked shocked and apprehensive, but Charlie knew he was all right. That was one good thing about the Camera Club. You could always say what you thought, and Mr Feinstein would take it seriously.

He considered Charlie's question. 'However you put those pictures up, people will look for a pattern. They'll try to make the arrangement mean something, so you might as well be in control of that. Offer them your own overview.'

Charlie looked down at the photographs on the table, trying to see what Mr Feinstein meant, but he couldn't. They were just a heap of separate pictures. When he looked up again, Mr Feinstein was grinning.

'Give it time. You'll agree with me in the end.' He heaved himself out of the chair. 'But stick to my plan until you do. I've got to go and talk to Mr Milverton now. Think you can cope on your own?'

'Of course we can,' Jennifer said. She knelt down beside the coffee table and began to sort the pictures into tidy piles, as Mr Feinstein disappeared into the Head's office.

'What are you doing?' Charlie said.

'I'm sorting them into "ordinary" and "weird".' Jennifer picked up his river picture and stared at it. 'This is certainly one of the weird ones. How did you ever get an idea like that?'

Charlie grinned. 'You ought to read a few photography magazines. They'd soon get your head buzzing. Want me to lend you some?'

'Thank you,' Jennifer said. Not sounding very interested. She picked up another handful of photos and glanced at the display board. 'Can you sort out the drawing pins while I'm doing this?'

Charlie thought he must have misheard. 'Sort out the *drawing pins?*'

'They're not spaced evenly. If we leave them like that, they'll make the whole display look untidy.'

Charlie thought she was being ridiculous, but rearranging drawing pins was simpler than making conversation. He went to the board and began levering out pins with his thumbnail.

He'd put about half of them back—carefully measuring the distance between them—when he heard a faint noise behind him, as if Jennifer had caught her breath. He didn't know, afterwards, whether that had distracted him, or whether it was something completely different, but what happened next was very odd.

He positioned his next pin and pressed it in with a flourish. Straight through his finger.

He actually watched himself do it. His left hand was spread along the edge of the mounting sheet, holding it taut, with the thumb and forefinger lying on the paper. And he jabbed the pin through the flesh of his forefinger and into the board.

He just managed not to scream, but he couldn't stop himself wincing. Feeling sick, he slid the nails of his other hand under the head of the pin and pulled it free.

'Hey—' he began, spinning round.

Look what I did, he was going to say. Making a joke of it, in case Jennifer had heard him catch his breath. But the words dissolved in his mouth, because it wasn't Jennifer standing behind him.

She was away to one side, watching with a frown. Charlie was facing the boy he'd seen yesterday. The small, bony boy with the baggy uniform and the sticking-out ears. He was gazing at Charlie with steady, unblinking eyes.

Charlie found himself yelling. Holding out his bleeding, punctured finger and shouting at the top of his voice.

'Look at that! Look what you made me do!'

The moment the words were out, he knew they were nonsense. He'd had his back to the boy. Hadn't even known he was there. That irritating stare couldn't possibly have affected what he'd done with the pin.

But his own voice jangled uncomfortably in his head, echoing those other ridiculous words that had come out of the crowd on the field.

He made her fall off the wall.

He made her!

'I didn't,' the boy said harshly. Almost under his breath. 'I didn't do anything.'

Charlie waited for him to turn and go away, but he didn't move. Instead, he dropped his eyes to look down at the table. Staring and staring, as if he were mesmerized by the photograph on top of the 'weird' pile.

Charlie's black and orange picture.

Jennifer stepped forward and nudged him, digging her elbow into his skinny side. 'You're not supposed to be hanging round here. You'll get into trouble.'

'I got lost,' the boy mumbled. 'I was looking for the library.'

Taking him by the shoulders, she spun him round. 'It's down that corridor. Now stop bothering us. And keep out of trouble.'

He stared up at her for a minute, as if he thought she might say something else. Then he stumbled off down the corridor.

Charlie sucked his finger. 'You were a bit hard on him, weren't you?' Jennifer just shrugged, but he didn't give up. He'd never heard her talk to anyone like that before. 'Do you know him?'

'He's my brother,' Jennifer said shortly.

She turned away, to the display board, and began to pull out the pins he had just pushed in.

'What are you doing now?' Charlie said.

Her voice was expressionless. 'There's blood on the paper. We'll have to turn it round and put the photos on the other side.'

Chapter Three

The display was meant to stay up until after half term. But sometime in the middle of October, Charlie's picture disappeared.

He walked through the foyer one morning, and the gap screeched out at him. Jennifer had arranged the whole display very skilfully, so that people's eyes were drawn in towards the middle, and she had put Charlie's picture right in the centre. Now it had vanished, and everything focused on an empty space.

Charlie charged straight along to the staffroom and banged on the door. Mrs Ramm, the librarian, came to open it.

'No need to make so much noise,' she said drily. 'We're not deaf in here.'

'Sorry.' Charlie tried to peer round her, 'Is Mr Feinstein there?'

Mrs Ramm shook her head. 'He's away on a course. He won't be back until after half term. Is it important?'

'One of my photographs has gone. From the display in the foyer. I wondered if Mr Feinstein had taken it.'

'I expect so.' Mrs Ramm looked carefully at Charlie. 'Do you want me to leave him a message?'

Charlie shook his head and backed away. What message could he leave? *My photograph's been stolen?* That would sound stupid. Especially if Mr Feinstein had taken it down himself. It would be easier to forget the whole thing and have another print made.

There was nothing urgent about that—except that the picture stuck in his mind. He took the negative into the chemist's on the Monday of half term, first thing in the morning.

Then he went on to meet Keith at the swimming pool. Zoë and Rachel were there too, and they all went to McDonald's and had a burger for lunch. It was three o'clock by the time he got home.

When he walked into the house, there was a lot of rustling and banging coming from his bedroom, and the door was wide open. All his copies of *Practical Photography* and *Photo Answers* were stacked up on the landing.

'What's going on?' he called, as he ran upstairs.

His mother crawled out from behind his bed. 'I'm cleaning. Ever heard of that? You could do it yourself, if you tried.'

'But what about my magazines? Why are they out here?'

Mrs Willcox sat back on her heels. 'Because they're in the way, that's why. And I promised Zoë I'd find her some magazines for her homework. She needs pictures of the countryside.'

'She's not cutting them out of my magazines!' Charlie yelped.

'Why not?'

'I need them!'

'Oh, come on.' His mother rolled her eyes up at the ceiling. 'You never even look at them. They just lie around your room in heaps.'

'I do read them! And anyway, Zoë can't have them, because—' A vague memory floated into Charlie's head, and he snatched at it. 'I've promised to lend them to someone in the Camera Club.'

His mother's eyes narrowed. 'You told me everyone else *had* those magazines. That was why I ordered them for you.'

'Everyone does have them,' Charlie said quickly. 'Except Jennifer. She's only just joined, and I promised I'd lend her some.'

Mrs Willcox looked doubtfully at the magazines.

'Can I put them back in my bedroom?' Charlie said. 'Please?'

'No, you can't!' Mrs Willcox jumped to her feet. 'If she really wants to borrow them, you can take them round now.'

She scooped up a huge bundle of magazines and tottered downstairs to dump them in her shopping trolley. Then she looked up at Charlie.

'Right! Get the rest down here. I want them out of the house.'

'What . . . straight away?'

'Now or never.'

'Well . . . I'll have to look up her address.' Charlie carried another armful of magazines downstairs and crammed them into the trolley as well. Then he slid into the sitting room and picked up the phone book.

He didn't need to take the magazines to Jennifer's. It would be simple to hide them at Keith's, until his mother's cleaning blitz had died down. But when he looked in the phone book, there were only two families called Luttrell, and one of them lived too far away to be Jennifer's.

He went out into the hall again and looked at the shopping trolley. His mother was pushing in the rest of the magazines, and it was overflowing. Keith would laugh himself silly if he turned up with that. And he wasn't very keen on the Camera Club at the best of times. The magazines might be safer if they really were at Jennifer's.

Charlie picked up his jacket. 'OK. I'm off.'

'Great!' his mother said triumphantly. She opened the front door and waved him through.

He trundled off with the trolley, heading across town, towards the Old Bridge. Jennifer lived on the other side of the bridge, on River Walk. Not too far along, he hoped. After half a mile or so, the road swung away from the river and turned into a long, steep hill. It wouldn't be much fun pulling a heavy trolley up there.

He was in luck. Number eighty-nine was quite near the bridge, next to a long alley that ran down to the river. Charlie peered between the high garden walls that closed the alley in, and saw a muddy footpath running along the bank. And, beyond that, across the river, the untidy, ugly back of Kenworthy's department store. Five floors of brick, covered in drainpipes.

The Luttrells' house made a startling contrast to that. It was immaculate. The garden wall had just been repointed, the paint on the house was spick and span. At the side, a gleaming black wrought-iron gate led through into the back garden. Even the path at the front looked newly scrubbed.

As Charlie dragged his trolley up the front path, its wheels scattered squashed brown leaves over the crazy paving. He scuffed them sideways, on to the weedless flower bed, and rang the bell. It trilled like a robin.

Jennifer opened the door, and Charlie grinned at her, before she could look surprised.

'I've brought those photography magazines I promised you.'

He started to pull his trolley over the threshold, into the house. Jennifer caught her breath.

'The wheels—'

'Oh. Sorry.' Charlie hadn't thought about mess. Even when his mother was having a cleaning blitz, she didn't fuss about little things like dead leaves.

But then his parents would never have bought a pale cream carpet like the one that stretched down Jennifer's hall. It must be a nightmare living with something like that. Charlie parked the trolley safely to one side of the door and pulled out an armful of *Photo Answers*.

'Where do you want them? Shall I dump them by the door?'

'No . . . I don't think—'

Jennifer looked as if she might be going to refuse them, but Charlie had no intention of letting her do that. He didn't like to think what would happen if he had to take them home again. He dropped them into her hands, so that she had to take them, and picked up another load.

'Where shall I put these?'

'I suppose they'd better go in my bedroom.' Jennifer turned towards the stairs, looking slightly shell-shocked.

'Fine,' Charlie wiped his feet on the doormat and followed her, determinedly.

They were almost at the top of the stairs when a door opened below them, and a woman's voice called out.

'Come down here! Look at all this mess you've made!'

Charlie stopped dead and looked guiltily over his shoulder, imagining a line of black footprints. But the cream carpet was still spotless.

'Peter!' the voice called. 'Hurry up! Daddy will be home soon!'

A door creaked on the landing, and a skinny figure shot out of one of the bedrooms and scuttled downstairs. If he recognized Charlie, he didn't give any sign of it. He ran straight into the kitchen, leaving the door open.

'Quick!' said the voice. It sounded very tense and sharp. 'Get the mop!'

'Mum!' Jennifer called warningly.

There was an abrupt silence, and then Mrs Luttrell came through the kitchen doorway and looked up at them, through the banisters. When she saw Charlie, she smiled nervously and patted her hair.

'Oh. Hallo. I didn't hear the bell.'

She was as small and frail-boned as a bird. Charlie smiled back at her. The Polite Charming Smile that he saved for other people's mothers.

'Hi.'

'Charlie's lending me some magazines,' Jennifer said quickly. 'We're just putting them in my room.'

Mrs Luttrell tilted her head back and smiled again. A bright, brittle smile. 'You should have told me he was coming, Jenny. I'd have made a cake.'

Oh no. Charlie could see she was going to make the whole thing into a performance. He gave her another burst of the PCS. 'That's really kind of you, Mrs Luttrell, but Jennifer didn't know I was coming. I'm just dropping these off.'

Mrs Luttrell's hands fluttered restlessly. Like Peter's. 'You must have a drink, at least. I'll call you in a minute.'

'Honestly,' Charlie said, 'you don't need to bother—'

But she had already vanished into the kitchen.

Charlie followed Jennifer into her bedroom. That was just as immaculate as the rest of the house. All the books on the shelves looked brand-new, and there was a row of soft toys on the frilly white duvet. Arranged with precision. Charlie grinned and spoilt the tidiness by dumping his armful of magazines on to the bed.

19

The top one caught his eye, and he picked it up again. 'There's a great article on portraits in this. It'll make you take a whole new look at your brother.' He grinned again, and began to leaf through, hunting for it.

'I'll just fetch the rest of the magazines first,' Jennifer said, already half-way through the door. 'Is it all right if I leave your trolley outside?'

'Fine,' Charlie said. 'As long as it doesn't make your front garden too untidy.'

The joke was wasted. Jennifer gave him a blank stare and disappeared. Charlie looked at his reflection in the mirror and groaned.

No wonder she was so uptight. The whole house was organized to death. Even the front garden was on parade, and he was ready to bet that the back was just as bad. Dropping the magazine he was holding, he strolled across the room and looked out of the window.

He was right. There was a long, bare lawn, meticulously cut, with a neat flower bed down each side. He couldn't spot a single dead leaf on the grass or a single weed among the carefully spaced dahlias. It wasn't a garden to play in.

Even the shed, at the far end of the garden, was newly creosoted. The late afternoon sun glinted on its single, polished window and on the gleaming brass padlock on its door. Behind it, the laurel bushes along the back wall were pruned into geometric shapes and the wooden gate was painted snow-white.

But beyond the gate—

Charlie almost laughed out loud.

Chapter Four

Beyond the back gate, the tidiness stopped. Bang. The whole careful, ultra-tidy view was completely ruined by the river that sprawled behind the wall, making a joke of the Luttrells' garden.

The muddy footpath along the nearer bank was littered with fallen leaves. The bank on the other side was a tangle of brambles and lurching willow trees, and two of the willows had collapsed into the river, snagging a mess of cans and carrier bags on their branches. Downstream, the willows gave way to tall, elegant beech trees, but the view was no better. Through the beeches loomed the back of Kenworthy's, as ugly and shabby as a warehouse.

Hurrah! thought Charlie.

Catching the sound of Jennifer's feet on the stairs, he turned away from the window before she could catch him snooping. As he turned, something odd caught his eye, a tiny peculiarity that he hadn't noticed before. It wouldn't have been remarkable anywhere else, but in that perfectly organized garden it stood out like a snowman in August.

'Someone's left the key in that padlock.' He waved his hand at the little brown shed. 'You'll lose your lawnmower if you're not careful.'

'It's all right,' Jennifer didn't even glance through the window. 'That's where it goes.'

'Not much point in locking the shed if you leave the key. Unless you're trying to stop the lawnmower getting out.'

'It's all *right*.'

This time, there was an edge to Jennifer's voice. Avoiding Charlie's eyes, she walked across to the bed and dropped the rest of the magazines on to the pile. Her hand hovered over them.

'Is there anything in any of them about . . . ' she hesitated. ' . . . about taking pictures at night?'

'At night?' Charlie frowned. 'Is that what you want to do?'

'I . . . might.' Jennifer ran a finger across the cover of the top magazine, avoiding his eyes.

'Sounds interesting,' Charlie said hopefully. But Jennifer didn't respond.

Oh well, if she wanted to be mysterious, let her get on with it. He wasn't going to pry. He began to rummage in the pile of magazines.

'I think there's an article in last November's *Photo Answers* . . . '

He flopped on to the bed and burrowed. As he found the article, he remembered a second one and he was hunting for that when a voice called from the stairs.

'Jennifer! I'm ready!'

Jennifer was reading the first article that Charlie had given her. She looked up sharply. 'We'll come straight down,' she called back.

But she wasn't quick enough. Before she had finished speaking, Mrs Luttrell's face appeared round the door.

'I've made some scones and—oh!' Her eyebrows went up and her eyes darted from the magazines scattered on the floor to the others heaped beside Charlie and Jennifer on the bed.

Jennifer jumped up. 'It won't take me a minute to tidy them.'

Mrs Luttrell laughed lightly. 'Don't say it like that. Charlie will think I'm an ogre.' But she didn't tell Jennifer to stop tidying. 'Come down when you're ready. I'll put the scones out.'

Groan, thought Charlie. But he could see there was no escape. He helped with the tidying and then followed Jennifer downstairs.

He could hardly believe his eyes when they walked into the dining room. Mrs Luttrell must have made the scones specially. They were little round ones, with frilly edges. Still warm. And she'd put out a plate full of butter curls and a china dish of strawberry jam. And honey in a pot shaped like a beehive.

'Wow!' Charlie said politely.

Mrs Luttrell gave a small, gratified smile. 'A cup of tea?'

'No thanks.' He hated tea.

Mrs Luttrell obviously hadn't expected that. She began to flutter apologetically. 'Coffee? Orange juice? Lemon squash?'

Charlie thought quickly. Coffee and juice sounded like bad ideas. He could imagine endless fuss about grinding beans or squeezing oranges. 'Lemon squash, please.'

Mrs Luttrell raised her voice. 'Peter! Bring a glass of lemon squash!'

There was a shuffle in the kitchen. Then the sound of a tap running.

'Careful!' Mrs Luttrell called. 'Don't spill it!'

When Peter pushed the door open, Charlie saw, instantly, that he'd filled the glass too full. He was carrying it with the sort of tense concentration that meant he was sure to slop it when he put it down.

'Thanks,' Charlie said brightly. He jumped up to take the glass and then stood back, to leave a way through to the empty chair.

Briefly, Peter hesitated, glancing at his mother, and Charlie realized that there was no plate in front of the fourth chair. Mrs Luttrell waved her hand quickly.

'Sit down, then. Don't keep everyone waiting.'

Peter wriggled into the chair, catching the edge of the table with his knees and jerking the cloth. Charlie put a hand on it, to stop it sliding off, relieved that Mrs Luttrell had just turned away to take a plate out of the sideboard.

'There you are,' she said, handing it to Peter. 'Now be careful. I don't want jam on the cloth. And don't put your elbows on the table.'

That was how it went on. Every time Peter moved, his mother stiffened nervously and nagged him. *Mind the cup! Not too much jam!* After ten minutes or so, Charlie couldn't bear it any longer. The only thing to do was provide a distraction.

'Have you heard what we go through at the Camera Club, Mrs Luttrell?' He grinned at Jennifer and launched into his famous Mr Feinstein impression. 'These photographs are prissy rubbish! Not fit for anything except *chocolate boxes*! I want pictures with *GUTS*!'

'Goodness!' Mrs Luttrell said, breathlessly.

'It was even worse last week.' Charlie wagged a finger ferociously. 'You're all *blind*! But I'm going to *CURE* you! If you want to stay in this club, you must choose a subject for a photo essay by the end of term. And it had better be good, because you'll be working on it for the rest of the year. So get out there and *open your eyes*!'

Mrs Luttrell swallowed. 'He sounds terrifying.'

'He's great,' Charlie said cheerfully. 'He tells you just what he thinks, with no messing about. And when he's got you feeling useless, he suddenly says, *I like it!*—and you know you've done something brilliant.'

'Like your river picture,' said Peter, under his breath.

Mrs Luttrell frowned at him. 'Sssh!'

Charlie didn't see why Peter couldn't join in. He turned and smiled at him. 'My river picture?'

Peter hung his head, mumbling down at the cloth. 'The night one. From the Old Bridge.'

'Oh, that.' Charlie grinned. 'Yes, Mr Feinstein really liked that. He—' Then he realized what an odd thing Peter had said. He looked curiously at him. 'What makes you think it's the Old Bridge? There's nothing in the photo except water and light.'

Peter shrugged and stared at the cloth until his mother prodded him. 'Don't be rude! Answer Charlie when he asks you a question!'

Peter frowned. 'You were on a bridge,' he said slowly, 'because your shadow's in the middle of the water. And . . . ' His face cleared suddenly, as if he'd just worked it out. 'And the New Bridge has more street lamps than that. They make a strip of light, not a patch.'

Charlie shook his head, admiringly. 'You know the river pretty well, don't you? I've never noticed that. Do you go fishing?'

'Certainly not!' Mrs Luttrell said. She gave Peter a suspicious look. 'He's not allowed down by the river.'

Peter ducked his head, so that his face was hidden, but the tips of his ears flamed scarlet and Charlie felt a twinge of guilt. He hadn't meant to get him into trouble.

'They sometimes take the Year Sevens out on river walks,' he said, inventing quickly. 'It stops them littering the school up.'

Mrs Luttrell's face relaxed a little. 'Well, I hope they keep an eye on Peter, or he'll fall in.' She reached across the table and prodded him again. 'Pass Charlie another scone. Can't you see his plate's empty?'

'No, really,' Charlie said. 'I couldn't—' But Peter's hand was already moving towards the plate of scones.

And then there was the sound of a key in the front door.

Immediately, all the Luttrells sat up straighter. Jennifer smoothed the table cloth, Mrs Luttrell reached for another cup and saucer and began to pour some tea, and Peter glanced nervously over his shoulder, still holding the plate of scones. The room was full of tension as the front door closed and a man's footsteps came down the hall.

Charlie was expecting a monster. Someone six foot tall, with bushy eyebrows and a scowl. It was all he could do not to grin at the contrast when the dining room door swung open. Mr Luttrell was thin and slight, with a bony, nervous face. He nodded stiffly to Charlie.

'Hallo.' Then he looked sideways, at Peter. 'Why are you waving that plate around? Put it down.'

When Peter didn't react at once, his voice sharpened.

'Come on, boy! Put it *down*.'

Peter froze, as if he were paralysed, and his eyes glazed over. He wasn't looking at his father any more. He was looking through him, with a fixed, unnerving stare.

Mrs Luttrell started to flap. 'Don't be silly, Peter. Put it down.' She picked up the extra cup of tea and leaned across the table, holding it out to Mr Luttrell. 'Have some tea, dear.'

Mr Luttrell turned abruptly, away from Peter's eyes, and his elbow caught the teacup. It tipped sideways, splashing tea all over his trousers.

There was a second of horrified silence. Mr Luttrell's face went white with anger.

'Look what you've done now!' he hissed at Peter. 'As if I hadn't got enough to worry about—'

'I thought he was going to explode,' Charlie said, swirling the last half inch of coffee in his mug. 'But he didn't. He just . . . looked. I'd hate it if Dad looked at *me* like that.'

He felt sick remembering Mr Luttrell's icy rage and the stupid, paralysed expression on Peter's face.

'People get annoyed by different things,' Charlie's mother said lightly. She was sitting cross-legged, painting her toenails. On the kitchen table, because the light was better there. 'Dad doesn't care about spilling tea, but he'd be furious if you threw stones at Mrs Jeavons's cat.'

'But he wouldn't look as if . . . as if he hated me.' Charlie swallowed. 'And you wouldn't go all fluttery and apologetic, like Mrs Luttrell. It wasn't even Peter's fault, but she pushed him into the garden, to get him out of the way. As if—'

He looked up and saw his mother watching him. She was listening properly now, so he said what was in his head, even though it sounded silly.

'It felt as if she was *protecting* Mr Luttrell. From Peter.'

'Or from what Peter might make him do?' Mrs Willcox said. Charlie frowned, not understanding, and she smiled ruefully. 'Not everyone can handle being angry.'

Charlie wasn't sure he understood that either, but before he could get her to explain, heavy feet came thundering up the front path. There was a thud against the door and Zoë yelled through the letter box.

'Hallo! It's us!'

Rachel was close behind. Lighter on her feet, but not so fast. 'Can we come and get some conkers?' she called.

Mrs Willcox pulled a face and screwed the top back on to her nail varnish. 'I hadn't even noticed the conkers were ripe. Where does the year get to? It'll be the fireworks party before we can turn round. Go and let them in, Charlie.'

Chapter Five

'Conkers!' Mr Feinstein said with relish.

He turned his paper bag upside down. Dozens of new, shiny conkers rolled across the table and on to the floor and half the Camera Club started crawling after them.

Mr Feinstein ignored that. Scooping up the nearest conkers, he held them out, in cupped hands. 'Here's a little exercise, to keep you busy while you're choosing subjects for your photo essays. I'll give a free roll of film for the best picture connected with conkers.'

Yes! Charlie thought. That was just his sort of thing. Usually, Mr Feinstein's competitions were arty and difficult. Sunsets and still life arrangements. He hadn't got a clue about those, but he did know how to take pictures of people, especially when they weren't expecting it.

Mr Feinstein was busy arranging his conkers into a gleaming pyramid on the table. He looked up and caught Charlie's eye.

'This would make an interesting still life, Willcox. Look at the way they reflect the light.'

'Bit of an obvious angle, isn't it?' Charlie knew when he was being teased. 'A moron could invent that, with his eyes shut.'

It was another Feinstein quote. Mr Feinstein grinned back at him. 'You're going to produce something better, are you?'

Charlie pushed his hands into his pockets and looked at the people scrabbling for conkers on the floor. 'Something different, anyway. I don't want to fiddle around in here. I'd rather get outside and take some action shots.'

'The Conker League?' Mr Feinstein placed the last conker delicately on top of his pyramid. 'Great idea! *If* you can pull it off.'

It was a dare, but Charlie didn't care. He didn't want to mess around making pretty arrangements on a table. He wanted something exciting.

It took him three days to find the right match. The Conker League was in full swing already, but he was looking for something with real tension. And he knew he'd found it when Zoë came in one evening and said she was lined up to play Felicity Rathbone.

There was a lot riding on the match. The conkers were both two hundreders, and Felicity was leading the League, with Zoë in second place. At break the next morning, half the school crowded into one corner of the playground to watch, and Richard Whitbread was very busy taking bets. With two lookouts posted in case of teacher trouble.

While Felicity and Zoë were getting ready, and sizing each other up, Charlie prowled round with his Pentax, deciding where to stand. It was no use going for the obvious shot, with both players in profile and the conkers clashing in mid-air. That would need split second timing and twenty tons of luck. He could take fifty shots and not get one quite right. There must be a better chance than that.

As the match started, he wormed his way in and out of the crowd, looking for another angle. After seven swings—three of Felicity's and four of Zoë's—he knew just what he wanted. The really interesting thing about the match was Zoë's expression. Felicity was a deadpan player, but Zoë's face showed everything: rage, relief, excitement. If he stood just behind Felicity's shoulder, he could take his picture just after Zoë's conker was hit, and catch her reaction.

If it worked, it would be brilliant.

He waited while Felicity lined up her swing rocking faintly backwards and forwards on the balls of her feet. Then, as she pulled back the conker, straining its string taut, he put his eye to the viewfinder. The instant he saw her let go, he pressed the button.

And Zoë screamed.

Charlie was concentrating on his shot and he didn't react for a moment. By the time he did, Zoë was surrounded by dozens of people, crowding round to ask questions and offer advice. Charlie craned his neck, trying to see between the heads and work out what had happened.

The conker had split at the moment of impact, shattering into flying fragments. One of them had shot straight up, into Zoë's eye. For a few seconds there was confusion. Then Zoë's voice bellowed above the chatter.

'I'm not dead. I'm not even blind. Leave me alone.' She charged out of the crowd with one hand held up to her face, elbowing people out of the way. As she passed Charlie, he caught at her arm.

'Zoë—'

'I'm OK!' she muttered fiercely. 'I'm not made of marzipan.'

He let her go. He guessed that she was trying to get inside before she burst into tears. Weeping in public wasn't much in her line. Maybe it was best to give her ten minutes on her own and then go and check that she really was all right.

Felicity Rathbone was still standing by the fragments of Zoë's conker, murmuring pathetically. 'I didn't mean to hurt her. I didn't know it would do that. I couldn't have stopped it.'

One or two people went to comfort her, but everyone else started drifting off, looking for some other entertainment. Charlie was wondering whether to take a picture of the broken conker when he noticed the group of girls off to one side, clustered round Rachel.

They were mostly in the same year as she was. But at the centre of the group was Skinny Martin's sister, Eleanor, from Zoë's class. The one with the sharp, weasel face.

She was whispering steadily, and the others were leaning in close to listen. Every now and again, they turned to look at the pieces of conker. Then they turned back, and Skinny's sister whispered a bit more.

There was something furtive about those backward glances. Charlie didn't know why, but they made him uneasy. He thought he might drift across and see what they were talking about.

But he didn't have time. With one last glance at the bits of conker, the whole crowd suddenly took off, heading briskly towards the school. Charlie hoped they were just going to help Zoë, but he didn't think so. They hadn't got the brisk, self-righteous air of girls playing Florence Nightingale. Rachel looked worried and miserable, and Eleanor Martin had an avid, unpleasant smile. He wondered if he ought to follow.

But just then Keith came running across the field, demanding to know what he'd missed. By the time Charlie had told him the whole story, the bell was ringing for the end of break.

Charlie looked at his watch. 'I think I'll just nip up to Zoë's classroom and make sure she's OK.'

'Of course she's OK,' Keith said, dismissively. 'Anyway, why are you fretting? She's only your cousin.'

Charlie didn't waste time explaining what 'cousin' meant in his family. He just pulled a resigned face and went to take a look in Zoë's tutor room. She wasn't there, but he found her just down the corridor in Rachel's, with a gaggle of Year Sevens. And Eleanor Martin.

'You all right, Zoë?' he called, from the doorway.

'Just about,' Zoë said. 'But it was a pretty peculiar accident. Wasn't it?' She gave him an odd, challenging look.

'Well . . . a bit strange, I suppose.' It didn't seem that peculiar to Charlie. 'But it couldn't be helped. Felicity was really upset. You ought to go and say something nice to her. It wasn't her fault.'

'Of course it wasn't *her* fault,' Zoë said.

She looked at Charlie, as if she were waiting for a question. When he didn't ask one, she glanced away from him, at Eleanor. Eleanor half-closed her eyelids, knowingly, and there was an indistinguishable mutter from the girls behind them.

Charlie waved a hand. 'As long as you're OK.'

Then he made off, as fast as he could. He hated huddles of whispering girls.

It was a week or so before he finished his film, and he'd almost forgotten about the conker picture by the time the prints were ready. But as soon as he looked through them, it jumped out at him.

He had captured the exact instant when the conker fractured. The fragments were blurred, but it was easy to see the separate pieces shooting away from the string, falling downwards or sideways or out towards the camera.

33

And it was easy to see the one, rogue piece flying upwards, past Zoë's open, disappointed mouth. Heading straight for her eyes.

He'd used a wide aperture, because he was concentrating on Zoë, and he wanted to cut out the background. That meant that most of the people behind had merged into a single blur.

But not all of them.

The crowd had been pressing in very close, and one face had moved into focus, just over Zoë's right shoulder. A narrow face that was gazing intently at the back of Zoë's head with a fixed, annoying stare. Intense, pale eyes.

Peter Luttrell.

Charlie looked at the picture for a long time, thinking of what Zoë had said about the accident. Remembering the huddle of girls in the classroom.

In the end, he put the print away in one of the folders on his desk. And he made himself a heap of conkers to photograph for Mr Feinstein's competition.

Chapter Six

But the other photograph nagged at his memory. He kept taking it out and looking at it. After a week or two, he forgot about hiding it and propped it on his desk, to look at while he was doing his homework.

That was how his mother came to see it.

He was struggling with his maths one evening, and she came in with a cup of coffee. 'You ought to stop. It's gone ten o'clock.'

'I'll be finished in a minute,' Charlie said. 'I think I've got the hang of these now.'

Mrs Willcox glanced over his shoulder. 'More than I could. They look impossible.' She leaned forward sharply. 'That's Zoë, isn't it?' Reaching past Charlie, she picked the print off the desk, before he could stop her.

'It's a conker picture,' he said quickly. 'Mr Feinstein had a competition.'

His mother peered at the photograph. 'You were actually taking this when the conker broke? You never said.'

'I forgot. Till I got the film back.'

Mrs Willcox held it closer. 'Who's this boy in the background? Glaring at her.'

'He's not glaring,' Charlie mumbled. 'That's just a trick of the light.'

'But who is it?'

Charlie picked up his coffee. 'Peter Luttrell.'

'The one whose father spilt his tea?' Mrs Willcox sounded amazed. 'That's not how I imagined him at all. I thought he was a pathetic, downtrodden little thing.'

'He *is* a pathetic, downtrodden little thing.' Firmly, Charlie took the picture back. 'That's just an odd shot.'

'Funny what cameras can do,' his mother said.

He thought that was the end of it. That she would go back downstairs and leave him to finish his homework. But the picture obviously niggled at her too. The moment he put it down, she picked it up again and walked across the room, to stand under the light.

'It's an irritating face, isn't it?' she said, after a moment.

'Zoë's?' said Charlie. Being deliberately obtuse.

'No, you pea-brain. That boy's. It's—' Mrs Willcox stopped, hunting for the right word. 'I don't know. Sullen. Secretive. It makes you want to shake him.'

'That's how everyone feels,' Charlie said drily. 'Must be really nice for him.'

'Mmm?' His mother wasn't really listening. She came back and put the picture down on the desk. 'Hasn't he got any friends?'

'How should I know?' Charlie slid the picture into his drawer and slammed it shut. 'Ask Rachel. He's in her class.'

His mother frowned. 'I don't see why you're getting so worked up. I only asked a simple question. You don't have to get angry just because I want to know about some odd-looking boy.'

'Sorry,' Charlie said. 'It's just that he seems to have a weird effect on people.'

The moment the words were out of his mouth, he knew they were disastrous. Now his mother would really start quizzing him. Asking all the questions he didn't want to think about. He shut his maths book and stood up.

'I think I'll go for a walk.'

'A walk? But it's pitch dark.'

'So?'

'What about your homework?'

'I'll finish it at school.' Charlie was through the door and half-way downstairs before she could say another word.

As he passed the dining room, he saw his father inside, bent over the table. The lamp made a pool of light in front of him and Charlie stopped for a second to watch his fingers moving deftly among the feathers.

He was tying trout flies. Choosing the right one and stripping off the section he wanted. Never hurrying. Never hesitating. Charlie had always been fascinated by how skilfully he did it. When he was a little boy, he had spent hours sitting at the other end of the table, wondering how his father's big hands could make something so small and perfect.

It would have been nice to go in there now. To sit quietly and watch, without having to talk. But it wouldn't last long. Once his mother realized where he was, she would be in there too. It was better to go out.

The moment he was through the front door, Charlie felt better. His mother had been wrong about the pitch dark. Even without the street lamps, there would have been plenty of light from the low, full moon. It was a clear night, so still that nothing except his feet rustled the dry leaves at the side of the pavement, and every sound seemed magnified by the moonlight. His own footsteps rang loud and ominous, and he could hear the sound of cars off to his left, in the small streets round the Castle. Behind that, faint and continuous, was the steady hum of traffic from the motorway, beyond the New Bridge.

He walked straight through the town, towards the Old Bridge. He meant to cross it and go up the hill towards Zoë and Rachel's house, but when he reached Kenworthy's he changed his mind. Instead of walking across the bridge, he turned right along the footpath that ran by the river.

It was a good, solitary place to be. The strip of trees between Kenworthy's and the river was only a hundred yards wide, but in the dark it felt like real woodland. The tall old beech trees towered over him, and the river whispered on his left, silver in the moonlight and black under the shadow of the trees.

He walked fast for ten minutes or so. Not thinking. Just enjoying the steady movement of his feet along the dry, level path. But then the beech trees gave way to drunken, disreputable willows and the path changed, zigzagging to avoid tangles of undergrowth. The ground was wet and muddy, and Charlie's feet slipped into sticky hollows.

For a few more moments he kept walking. Then he found his way blocked by a couple of fallen willows. Beyond them, the wood was much wilder and denser, and he came to a halt, not sure that it was sensible to go on.

And that was when he realized where he was.

Across the river, on the opposite bank, was the path that ran behind the houses of River Walk. And facing him, gleaming snow-white in the moonlight, was a wooden gate set in a high brick wall. Charlie could see the neat tops of the laurel bushes over the wall, and the pointed roof of the shed.

He hadn't consciously been heading for that spot, but he wondered whether his mind was taking revenge on him. He'd come out to avoid questions about the conker photograph and there he was, gazing across the river at Peter Luttrell's house. It didn't feel like an accident.

He didn't know how long he'd been standing there, staring at the wall, when he heard the noise. Maybe ten minutes, maybe longer. But suddenly, over the water, came a faint sound, carrying crisply in the still air.

A clack.

It came from beyond the high brick wall. A noise of wood smacking on wood, as if someone had pulled at a fence board and let it snap back into place. It wasn't a loud noise, but it was unexpected and automatically Charlie took a step forwards, to hide in the branches of the fallen willows.

There was another sound, even fainter. A scrabbling, scratching noise. Then a metallic clatter as something shook the white gate, rattling its catch.

And then, directly opposite Charlie, a dark shape slithered up on to the top of the gate. It flowed up in a single movement that was neither climb nor jump, but a strange mixture of the two, and Charlie's first thought was that it must be a cat.

But, almost before that idea was formed, he knew it was wrong. The legs were too short for a cat's and the body was too long. A small dog maybe?

It was hard to imagine the Luttrells with a dog. And there was something odd about the tail, too . . .

The creature didn't loiter on top of the gate for more than the instant it took to catch its balance. It flowed straight down the other side, on to the path, and then reared up on to its back legs, balancing with its tail.

And Charlie knew it was an animal that he'd never seen before.

It was silhouetted against the white gate, straining upwards to sniff the air. Its long body, balanced on the short back legs, would have reached above his knees, and the tail that propped it steady was thick and muscular. No dog had a tail like that. And no dog had such a small, rounded head, with ears set close against its skull.

For perhaps ten seconds, the creature stayed upright, turning its head from side to side to scan the river bank. Then it dropped on all fours and headed towards the water. The bank was high and steep on that side, and Charlie waited to see whether it would jump or clamber down.

It did neither. Instead, it slid, head first, down a strip of bank that was worn bare and smooth. There was hardly a sound as it hit the water, and it disappeared under the surface immediately.

A few seconds later, it came up, a hundred yards downstream. It was swimming fast, but the only thing that was visible above the water was the flattened top of its small, neat head. It would have been easy for Charlie to miss it altogether.

Except for the ripples it left behind, running out towards the bank on both sides in a wide V-shape.

Chapter Seven

What was it?

Charlie spent most of the next morning doodling in the margin of his rough book, attempting to draw what he'd seen, but he couldn't get it quite right. And he didn't have any luck discussing it with Keith, either.

'Cat,' Keith said. 'There's a couple living down by the river. Gone wild.'

Charlie knew it wasn't a cat. But when he started arguing, Keith yawned loudly, drowning him out. He kept his doodles to himself after that.

By lunch time, he was no nearer solving the problem. But when he was in the lunch queue, fighting his way towards the dining room, he saw a solitary figure coming the other way, struggling against the tide. It was Peter. He squeezed past Charlie, but instead of joining the queue he turned left, slipping into the library.

The library. Of course! Charlie couldn't believe he hadn't thought of it before. There was bound to be a picture of his animal in there somewhere.

For a second he hesitated, wondering whether it was worth losing his place in the queue. Then he caught the smell of stew, oozing up the corridor, and that made up his mind for him. No point in hurrying to eat *that*. There was sure to be plenty left, whenever he turned up.

Mrs Ramm was at her desk when he walked into the library. She looked up sharply, registered who he was and gave him a faint smile. Then she went back to her computer.

Charlie started working his way along the non-fiction shelves.

'Do you know what you're looking for?' Mrs Ramm said suddenly, from behind him.

Charlie spun round, feeling furtive. 'Just . . . something about nature. Wild animals.'

'Try the five hundred and nineties,' Mrs Ramm said briskly, as though he ought to have known the Dewey number without being told.

He waited until she bent her head again and then he walked down to the Natural History section at the far end of the library. It didn't take him long to find the right book, but it was heavy and unwieldy and he looked for somewhere to sit down.

That was when he saw the wall of books, on the far side of the furthest table. And behind the wall, hunched forward, he saw a small, bony figure with very short hair. Peter. He was already tucked away in a hidden corner, but he had made himself another defence with a set of encyclopaedias. If Charlie hadn't been right at the end of the library, he wouldn't have seen him at all.

He was tempted to avoid him, but most of the other tables were full, and he needed space for his book. As quietly as he could, he moved over to the table and settled himself on the opposite side. He started to leaf through the book, studying the pictures.

It didn't take him long to find what he was searching for. The image jumped straight out at him as he turned the page. Round head. Thick tail. Short, stumpy legs. There was even a sketch of the creature rearing upright, balancing on its hind legs and tail. Everything fitted.

But when he turned over, to read the description that matched the picture, it was quite different.

. . . elusive and nocturnal animals, now extremely rare, and absent from most parts of mainland Britain . . . live in or near rivers . . . swim underwater, with only the tips of their noses breaking the surface . . . hardly ever seen . . . characteristic droppings, or 'spraints', full of fish scales left on prominent boulders, tree roots, etc . . . their skulls are exceptionally fragile . . .

He read it twice, to make sure that he'd got it right. But there was no mistaking the message . . . *elusive . . . extremely rare . . . hardly ever seen . . .* There was no hint that they might have adapted to urban life, as foxes had. They just weren't the sort of animal you would see coming out of someone's back garden, in the middle of a town.

And yet . . .

He flipped back to the picture and there it was. Unmistakably. The animal he'd seen last night.

He frowned down at it, trying to think of a sensible answer, and as he did so he was suddenly aware of a smell. A smell that was so out of place in the library that he didn't recognize it at first. It was only when he shut his eyes and concentrated that he realized what it was.

Orange.

Someone was eating an orange, very close by. Breaking Mrs Ramm's strictest rule about not bringing food into the library.

Charlie opened his eyes and found himself being watched. Peter was staring at him over the wall of books, gazing steadily without any expression, as he lifted an orange segment towards his open mouth.

'Careful,' Charlie hissed. 'Mrs Ramm will go mad if she sees you.'

Peter didn't react at all. With his eyes fixed on Charlie's face, he posted the orange segment into his mouth. Staring.

Charlie began to feel uncomfortable. Not because the eyes were staring at him, but because they weren't. Peter was gazing straight across the table, but he was focusing somewhere else. He didn't seem to be looking out at the real world at all, but into some completely different space.

'Hey,' Charlie said abruptly. He had to produce a distraction, to get those unsettling eyes away from his face. Still watching Peter, because the idea of glancing away made him feel even more uncomfortable, he pulled an encyclopaedia out of the wall and sent his reference book sliding through the gap. 'Ever seen one of those?'

It was only a long shot, just in case Peter had caught sight of the animal too. He was totally unprepared for the reaction he got. Peter glanced down at the picture and drew his breath in, with a small squeak from the back of his throat. His mouth fell open and the piece of orange dropped out, half-chewed, and landed on the page in front of him.

'Oh, you idiot,' Charlie said. 'Don't let Mrs Ramm see *that*.'

But Peter didn't give any sign of having heard. He was gazing down at the picture as though it had hypnotized him. Charlie pulled out his handkerchief and stretched down the table, scooping up the horrible piece of orange without actually touching it. Then he stood up and walked towards Peter, intending to drop the orange into his lunch box.

And that was when Mrs Ramm chose to appear.

She stuck her head round the corner of the shelves and frowned. Charlie pushed the handkerchief into his pocket, orange and all, and flashed a smile at her, but it didn't work as well as usual. The frown stayed put.

'Have you found what you were looking for, Charlie?'

'I . . . yes, thanks.'

'Is there anything else you want? Or are you just annoying Peter?'

'*Annoying* him?' For a moment, Charlie was too startled to argue.

Mrs Ramm put a hand on his shoulder, forcing him round. 'If you've finished, you'd be better off outside.'

'Why? I haven't—'

Charlie looked down at Peter's bent head, waiting for him to say something. But he didn't. He just reached out a small, knobbly hand and closed the book. Then he put another piece of orange into his mouth.

Charlie turned on Mrs Ramm as she pushed him towards the door. 'You're not being fair! I wasn't doing anything!'

'Well, now you know what it's like for Peter,' Mrs Ramm said coldly. 'He doesn't do anything either.'

'He was eating!'

'That's my business.' Mrs Ramm sat down at her computer again, reaching for the mouse.

But Charlie wasn't ready to leave. He felt injured. Mrs Ramm was stiff and chilly, but he'd always thought she liked him. And he'd certainly never expected her to be unjust.

'I don't know why you picked on me,' he muttered. 'You know I don't go round annoying people. And Peter was the one who was breaking the rules.'

Mrs Ramm moved the mouse, clicked, and moved it again. For a second, Charlie thought she was going to ignore him completely. Then she said, very softly, 'A library isn't just a room full of books, you know. It can be a refuge too. For people who need somewhere to hide.'

She looked up.

'Yes,' Charlie muttered. 'OK. I see.'

Feeling stupid, he backed through the door and went to face the sad, stale stew. But he'd been wrong about that too. There wasn't any left, and he had to make do with a squashed cheese roll.

At least it was Thursday. That was his mother's day off, and she always cooked something special. When he pushed the kitchen door open, he was starving. He closed his eyes and sniffed the wonderful smell of onions and tomatoes and beans and chillies.

'How long till we eat?'

His mother grinned. 'It's your lucky day. We'll have to eat early, because Zoë and Rachel will be here.'

'All the evening?' Charlie pulled a face. He'd had enough of little kids for one day.

'Until Alison gets back from London,' Mrs Willcox said. 'Have you got anything they can do?'

'How about their homework?' Charlie said sweetly.

His mother stuck her tongue out at him. 'You're so welcoming!'

'Nothing wrong with homework,' Charlie said briskly. 'In fact, I'm off to do mine. Right now.'

He escaped upstairs while he could, shut the door firmly and turned on his radio. But he couldn't hide for ever. At half past five, Zoë stuck her head into the room and yelled.

'It's ready!'

Charlie turned the music off and she beamed at him, glowing with virtue.

'We laid the table, because you were busy. We did the salad too. And cooked the rice. But you have to come and carry the dishes in.'

'OK.' Charlie shut his folder and stood up.

Zoë smiled again. 'Mum always says it's hard on your mum, not having any girls to help her.'

'Don't you think that's sexist?' Charlie said.

Zoë tossed her head triumphantly. 'That's what I keep telling her. I think your parents ought to make you help.'

Charlie was tempted to tell her how much his mother hated people fussing round while she was cooking, but he decided it would be cruel. He ran downstairs and into the kitchen. 'I'll take the chilli through, shall I? Zoë's too little to manage that.'

There was a satisfactory snort from behind him. Cheerfully, he reached for the dish.

'Be careful,' his mother said. 'It's red hot.'

She was too late. Charlie whipped his fingers away from the dish and went to run them under the cold tap. Then he went back to the table, looking for a towel.

'Oh drat,' Mrs Willcox said. 'I've just put them all in the wash. Hang on and I'll get a clean one.'

'Don't bother. I'll use this.' Charlie pulled out his handkerchief.

As it flapped open, something dropped out, into the dish of chilli. Zoë pulled a face and squealed.

'Yuck!'

'What was that?' Mrs Willcox said.

Charlie opened the drawer and found a spoon. 'Nothing to fuss about. Just a bit of orange.'

His mother stared at him. 'Orange? In your hanky?'

'I took it off a kid in the library. So he wouldn't get into trouble with Mrs Ramm.'

That was enough of an explanation for his mother. She grinned and picked up the dish, as soon as he'd fished the orange out, but Zoë wasn't so easily satisfied. She was a school librarian, and proud of it.

'Someone was eating? In the library?' She turned to Rachel. 'That's strictly forbidden. Sin Number One.'

'I know,' Rachel muttered, going pink. Charlie guessed that she'd been caught at it herself, but Zoë missed the blush. She was too busy homing in on the piece of orange.

'Who was it?'

'Just one of the kids in Rachel's year.'

'Who?' Zoë said insistently.

Charlie hadn't meant to tell, but something—a flicker of resentment at how he had been treated, maybe—made him say, 'Jennifer Luttrell's brother.'

Rachel caught her breath. 'Evil Eye?' she whispered.

'*What?*' Charlie said.

Zoë grinned. 'Evil Eye. Everyone calls him that. Didn't you know?'

'Why?' said Charlie.

His voice was sharp. Zoë glared back at him, defiantly, and nudged Rachel. 'You tell him. It was your friends who invented it.'

'No it wasn't,' Rachel mumbled. 'It was your friend Eleanor. Because of the way he stares. And the way things . . . go wrong if he looks at you.'

Charlie had a sudden, unnerving memory of the drawing pin going into his finger. But he could hear Mrs Ramm's voice in his head as well. *Now you know what it's like for Peter. He doesn't do anything either.*

'That's all nonsense,' he said. 'You know it's nonsense, Rachel.'

Rachel nodded, sheepishly, and Zoë whisked round the table, to pick up the pile of plates.

'Of course we do, thicko. It's only a joke.'
But they avoided his eyes as they went out of the kitchen.

Chapter Eight

Now that he knew, Charlie could see that something was going on. Zoë had never been friendly with Eleanor Martin before, but now the two of them always seemed to be together. They'd gathered a little group of girls from Rachel's class and they huddled in corners at break, whispering to each other, with excited, self-important faces.

Charlie hoped there wasn't going to be trouble, but it didn't seem to be anything to do with him. Not until the Camera Club meeting, at the beginning of December.

It was a black, stormy day, with rain beating noisily against the windows. Charlie and Jennifer were heading for Mr Feinstein's room, and his voice came booming out to meet them.

'There are six of your things in this lost property box!' he bellowed. '*Six!*'

Jennifer pulled a face, and Charlie played an imaginary saxophone.

'It's those oh-ho-ho-ho-old lost property blu-u-u-ues.'

For most of the year Mr Feinstein ignored the lost property boxes that were kept in his room, leaving people to rummage if they wanted to. But every now and again the boxes overflowed and started invading the floor, and he went mad.

There was a mumble from the person he was shouting at, and then he yelled again.

'What do you mean it wasn't you? Did they run off by themselves? And jump into the box?'

'Lost Property Olympics!' hissed Charlie.

Jennifer smiled, but then she took another step forward and looked into the room, and her smile vanished abruptly. Charlie moved up beside her, to see why.

It was Peter in there.

He was standing very still and silent, with his head down, while Mr Feinstein flapped a bundle of clothes at him.

'Come on!' Mr Feinstein said impatiently. 'Speak! Or have you lost your tongue as well?'

Jennifer turned round, so quickly that she stepped on Charlie's toe. He gave a little squeal, half-joking, and Mr Feinstein glanced up and saw them in the doorway.

'Come on, then!' he called. 'You're late already. Where are the rest of you? And where are *you* going, Jennifer? Have you decided to leave the club?'

'I—' Jennifer went pink. She hadn't got a clue how to talk to Mr Feinstein. Charlie found himself chipping in, to save her from any more comments.

'We thought you were busy, sir.'

'Busier than I should be!' Mr Feinstein snapped. 'I'd have a lot more time for important things, if people didn't waste my time by littering their possessions round the school.'

He looked back at Peter, who was standing just as still and silent as before, and he obviously found that infuriating. Dropping the clothes on to his desk, he picked up a red exercise book and waved it so ferociously that the pages flapped.

'Haven't you missed this? Or have you given up physics? Hey?'

He flapped it again, and something fluttered out of the pages. A small, rectangular picture. Peter grabbed at it, but Mr Feinstein was too quick for him. He snatched it out of the air, and his eyes widened. Then he beckoned to Charlie.

'Willcox! I think this is yours.'

Puzzled, Charlie walked into the room and took the photograph that Mr Feinstein was holding out. Peter stood awkwardly silent, his fingers picking at the clothes on the desk. Charlie glanced down at the photograph.

It was his original black and orange river picture. The one that had been stolen.

'Well?' Mr Feinstein said, glaring at Peter. 'Don't you think you owe Charlie an explanation?'

The fingers stopped moving. Peter stood very still and Charlie looked at his bent head. At his clenched hands and the short, bristly hair at the nape of his neck. The bones were harsh knobs above the spotless shirt collar.

'He doesn't need to apologize,' Charlie said. Surprising even himself. 'I gave him the photograph.'

Peter glanced up, for a split second, and then dropped his head again. Mr Feinstein was speechless.

'You did . . . what?'

'I'm sorry,' Charlie smiled sunnily. 'I ought to have waited. But I knew you'd be taking the display down at half term, and Peter really liked that picture. So I gave it to him.'

Mr Feinstein took a long, deep breath. 'You told Mrs Ramm it had disappeared.'

Charlie's brain worked fast. He smiled again, very politely and charmingly, and told the truth. Almost. 'Oh, it turned up again. Didn't I tell you? And then I gave it to Peter.'

For a moment, he thought there was going to be an explosion after all. But Mr Feinstein just gave him a sour, disbelieving look and picked up the rest of Peter's lost property.

'OK, Luttrell. Get these out of my sight. And don't let me find you round the lost property box again, or there'll be trouble.'

Peter took the bundle and hesitated, glancing down at the photograph in Charlie's hand.

'It's all right,' Charlie said cheerfully. 'I really did mean you to have it.'

He tucked it into the clothes, and Peter bolted, wriggling his way out of the room with his possessions clutched to his chest. As the rest of the Camera Club flocked in, Charlie could hear him scuttling away down the corridor.

Mr Feinstein barely gave them time to sit down before he started. He was in a very bad temper now. 'Is everyone here?'

'Greg's away,' said someone.

'Well, tell him he has to come and see me, the minute he gets back. This is a crucial meeting, because you're all going to decide what to do for your photo essays.'

'Oh, *sir*!' There were protesting wails from all over the room. 'You didn't warn us!'

'That's not fair!'

Mr Feinstein folded his arms. 'It's perfectly fair. I've been warning you since the beginning of term, and it's the third of December today. If you haven't made up your minds by now, you never will. It's time for you to *commit yourselves*. And anyone who can't do that is out.'

There were a few more murmurs, but they all knew he never took any notice of complaints. After two or three seconds, the murmurs died away and everyone sat in silence. Waiting to see who would get picked on first.

'Willcox,' Mr Feinstein said, with relish.

Charlie had been expecting that. Mr Feinstein was getting back at him. If he didn't come up with a proper idea, he might really get flung out of the club.

He stalled for time. 'Yes, sir?' Inside his head, he was reviewing all his vague, half-formed notions about the photo essay, but it was hard to think with Mr Feinstein glaring like that.

'Come on, Willcox, what's it going to be? I want a proper idea. Not just funny pictures of your family.'

Everyone smirked. Charlie's family pictures were a standing joke at the Camera Club. As reliable and regular as Amy Mansfield's photos of her cat.

But Mr Feinstein wasn't teasing. He was taunting. Hassling. 'Well?' he said.

Charlie thought frantically, trying to work out what else he was good at, except for family pictures. He couldn't think of anything except the black and orange photograph that he'd just given to Peter.

Mr Feinstein frowned. 'If you haven't got a subject, you're OUT. I won't have time-wasters in this Club. If you can't—'

Charlie crossed his fingers and took a risk. 'I'm going to do the river,' he said.

Mr Feinstein stopped, in mid-rage. 'The river?'

'All round the town. Different places. Different times of year. Plants and animals and bridges. And the sewage works.'

The more he thought about it, the better it seemed. It was a proper subject, but he could do almost anything. Even funny family pictures, if they went for a walk by the river.

'Not bad,' Mr Feinstein said, in quite a different voice, and Charlie knew he was forgiven. He watched Mr Feinstein write his name at the top of a piece of paper. *C. Willcox— River.*

And that was when he had his wonderful, secret idea. An idea that made him want to grab his cameras and race straight down to the river.

If he could get a picture of the otter, his essay would be really special . . .

Chapter Nine

Jennifer waited for him at the end of the session. Not obviously loitering, but taking a long time to gather her things together, so that they reached the door at the same moment. Even then, she didn't speak straight away. But there was an awkwardness about her that showed she wanted to, so Charlie filled the gap.

'What subject did you choose?'

'Night,' she said. Very short and sharp.

Of course. He ought to have guessed. 'That's pretty tricky for a beginner.'

Jennifer shrugged. 'It's what I want to do.'

'So what sort of pictures will you take? Fireworks? Stars?'

'I thought . . . ' Jennifer looked down at her fingers. 'I thought I might try and photograph some animals. In the dark. Would that be very difficult?'

Charlie felt as if he'd had all the breath knocked out of him, but he tried not to show it. 'Any particular kind of animal?'

He thought he'd said it casually, but Jennifer's eyes snapped straight to his face.

'Why?'

'I . . . '

He didn't want to talk about the otter, because it was the best idea he'd got for his photo essay. But it seemed silly to keep it completely secret. He compromised.

'I was walking along the river a little while ago—on the other side from your house—and I saw something come over your garden wall.'

Jennifer's whole body went tense. 'What sort of something?'

'A . . . ' Charlie hesitated. 'An odd sort of animal. Not a dog or a cat.'

Jennifer half-closed her eyes.

'Have you seen it too?' Charlie said.

'Not *seen*,' Jennifer said slowly. 'But there's been something about. Trampling round the back gate at night, and leaving tracks.'

'What sort of tracks?'

'They're too blurred to make out really. My father thinks it's rats, but I'm not sure. That's why I wanted to get a photograph.'

'Sounds like a good idea.'

Jennifer frowned. 'But it's really difficult. I've tried already and I just fall asleep while I'm watching.'

'You can't do it like that. What you need is some sort of automatic switch. That the animal will set off when it passes.'

'Like a photo-electric cell?' Jennifer looked sarcastic. 'I can just see my parents coughing up the money for one of those.'

'Don't they want to see what the animal is?'

Jennifer snorted. 'They don't care what it is. They just want to get rid of it. My father's going to get the Pest Control Officer to come and put some poison down.'

A shiver went down Charlie's back. He remembered the strong, graceful otter. Its inquisitive head and the way it had launched itself into the water. 'He wants to kill it?'

'It's his garden,' Jennifer said defensively. 'And he doesn't like . . . things getting into it. He's got enough to worry about, without rats. Or whatever.'

She was on the verge of tears. Or anger. Charlie wasn't sure which, but he didn't want to find out. 'Whatever I saw, it

wasn't a rat,' he said cheerily. 'It was something much nicer.'
He grinned. 'If you get a picture, your father might decide to
tame it, instead of killing it. Maybe it'll end up sleeping on his
bed.'

Jennifer pulled a face. 'Not much chance of that. Our
house is barred to all non-human life.'

Her laugh wasn't very convincing, but she was trying to be
flippant. Charlie laughed too.

'How do you manage then? Does your father make you
sleep in the shed?'

It was just a silly insult. The kind of thing he might have
said to Zoë, or Keith. But Jennifer went bright red and her
eyes snapped.

'Why did you say that?'

'I . . . ' Charlie felt like an idiot. 'It was just a joke.'

'Oh. Yes.' Jennifer gave a forced laugh and turned away, as
if to end the conversation. But then she turned back, abruptly.
'I meant to say—thank you for getting Peter off the hook.
You didn't really give him that photograph, did you?'

Charlie shrugged. 'He can have it. I thought he could do
without any more hassle.'

'It's his own fault,' Jennifer said, stiffly. 'He shouldn't lose
things.'

'Maybe he didn't lose them,' Charlie said. Thinking about
it properly for the first time. 'The other kids pick on him,
don't they? I expect they helped his stuff into the lost
property box.'

'That's his own fault too,' Jennifer muttered. 'He's always
annoyed people, ever since he was little. He makes them
angry.'

'That's no excuse for bullying,' Charlie said firmly. 'He
doesn't do anything, does he?'

Jennifer shook her head. 'It's not what he does that causes trouble. It's what he *is*.'

She walked off down the corridor, before Charlie could work out what she meant.

He couldn't settle to his homework that evening. At ten o'clock he gave it up and went downstairs.

'I'm going out for a bit.'

'Again?' His mother looked up from her crossword. 'What's with all this roaming around at night?'

Charlie shrugged. 'I'll go and meet Dad, when he comes out of the pub.'

As soon as he'd said it, he knew it was a good idea. Pulling on a coat, he went out into the dark. The sky was clear and bright, with a scattering of stars, and every parked car was already pale with frost. The grass on the verges crunched under his feet.

He was too early. He could see his father through the window of the Half Moon, still chatting to his friends from the Angling Society. Charlie didn't feel like going inside, so he strolled up and down, watching his breath in the cold air.

He was right at the far end of the road when the men came out of the bar. They set off in a gaggle, with Mr Willcox in the centre, and Charlie had to jog after them.

'Dad!'

They all turned, and his father tilted his head, to peer past the light from the pub. 'Charlie?'

There was a burst of slow, amiable laughter.

'Poor lad. Has to come and fetch his father home.'

'Do it every night, do you, Charlie?'

The men stopped and waited, standing slightly apart, so that Charlie could come into the middle of the group. That wasn't what he wanted, and he hung back awkwardly. Without any fuss, the men picked that up and began to drift off, nodding to his father.

'Better get home.'

'See you next week, Rob.'

Mr Willcox waited until they had all gone. Then he walked down to meet Charlie. 'Everything all right?'

'Fine,' Charlie said. And then stopped, because he didn't know how to explain himself.

Mr Willcox looked down at his watch. 'Fancy a turn round the block before we go home? I could do with a bit of air.'

'Good idea.' Charlie tried to sound as relaxed as his father. 'Where shall we go?'

'Where d'you fancy?'

The answer seemed inevitable. 'The river?'

'Annoying all the courting couples?' Mr Willcox chuckled. 'All right. Why not? Haven't got your good shoes on, have you?'

It wouldn't have mattered if he had. The mud on the river bank was frozen hard and dry. And it was too cold for courting couples. Side by side, the two of them strolled down the side of the Half Moon and on to the Jubilee Walkway.

The river banks had been cleared on both sides, to make wide stretches of grass, laced with concrete paths and dotted with benches and litter bins. Apart from one or two carefully placed trees, there was nothing to interrupt the view across the river.

They walked in silence. Charlie half expected his father to give him a lead by asking questions, but he didn't. He just walked easily in the dark, comfortable and quiet.

They followed the curve of the river round past the end of the Walkway, to the castle, where the old houses rose straight from the bricked up banks. The New Bridge swooped over them, and they stood under its arch, listening to the noise of cars passing overhead on their way to the motorway. Mr Willcox rested his arms on the railings and gazed out at the dark water.

And suddenly it was easy. 'Dad?'

'Mmm?'

'Have you ever seen an otter?'

His father laughed, softly. 'That's a bit of a sore point.'

'What do you mean?'

Mr Willcox laughed again, and rubbed his forehead. 'When I was a lad, my mates used to tease me about otters. They'd come in with tales about spraints, and send me scurrying up and down the river. Miles, sometimes. But I never caught sight of one. And I don't suppose I ever shall now.'

'Why not? You're always down by the river.'

'Oh, *I'm* here.' Mr Willcox turned and leaned back, with his elbows on the rail. 'But the otters aren't. Haven't been any on this stretch of river for years.'

'None?' Charlie stared out at the river. At the wide strip of orange reflected from the lights on the bridge. 'There's a friend of mine that reckons he saw an otter,' he said slowly. 'Very near here.'

He held his breath, waiting for questions, but there weren't any. His father just grinned. 'Mink.'

Charlie looked up. 'What do you mean?'

'Plenty of mink around. Nasty little devils. They've wiped out all the water voles round here. People see them and start jabbering about otters, because they've forgotten how big real otters are.'

Charlie wasn't going to argue, but he knew it wasn't a mink he'd seen. He had studied the measurements in the book and his animal was much longer.

'What about . . . pets?'

'Pet mink?' His father snorted. 'Why would anyone want one of those? They're vicious little beasts. And they stink.'

'No, I meant—'

'Otters?' Mr Willcox reached over and tugged Charlie's ear. 'This isn't the wilds of Scotland, you know. If anyone had an otter round here, it would be famous.' He heaved himself upright and looked at his watch. 'Better get back. Mum'll be fretting.'

They climbed the flight of steps that led up on to the bridge, and Charlie took a last look down at the water. Something—the pattern of orange light, that wasn't like the light by the Old Bridge—made him think of Peter.

'There's a boy at school who gets called Evil Eye,' he said, abruptly. 'People reckon things go wrong if he stares.'

'Not very nice,' Mr Willcox said. 'Someone you know?'

'Sort of. His sister's in my class. He's only eleven or twelve.'

Charlie could feel his father watching him, but he didn't turn round. He went on staring at the water, and the steady, smooth way it flowed under the bridge. Trembling like black and orange silk.

'Come on,' Mr Willcox said at last. 'Time we went home. It's turning colder. Might even get some snow later on.'

They began to walk back through the town, past the castle. 'Do you think there's anything in that stuff?' Charlie said. 'About the evil eye?'

'Load of rubbish,' said his father. Just as Charlie had known he would. 'Silly kids trying to scare themselves.' He glanced sideways. 'It's pretty rough on that boy, though. Someone ought to watch it doesn't turn nasty.'

'Yes,' Charlie said. 'Yes, someone should.'

Chapter Ten

But he was more interested in the otter than he was in Peter. He needed to get started on his photo essay, and that wasn't as easy as he'd expected.

He spent two or three weeks slowly working his way round the loop of the river without getting any inspiration. Going clockwise from his own house, along the Jubilee Walkway to the New Bridge and the castle and then on, past the school and the Old Bridge. He was hunting for ideas and watching for the otter, but all he got was chilblains and a bad cold.

And all his pictures looked dreadful. Silly little views of the Old Bridge and the ruins of Toller's Mill, like picture postcards, without sunshine. He didn't know what to do.

Then, in the last week before Christmas, he stayed behind at the end of an English lesson and found himself walking down empty corridors, after everyone else had gone out for break. As he passed the cloakrooms, he heard a peculiar noise. Half snort and half giggle.

He ignored it and walked on, but when he was almost at the corner, it came again, sounding even odder. He turned and walked back, slowly and quietly. Tiptoeing into the cloakroom, he peered round the end of the line of coats.

Peter was right down at the far end of the cloakroom, under the window, with his back to a radiator. His face was as stiff as a plaster cast, but his eyes glittered. He was staring off towards the left.

Charlie waited, wondering what was going on.

Suddenly, Peter took a step forward. Immediately, three girls moved out of the shelter of the hanging coats, barring his way. They had their backs to Charlie, and he couldn't see who they were, but they were around Peter's age. Each one was spinning a shiny conker, on a long black bootlace.

Walking slowly towards Peter, they began flicking their conkers. Closer and closer, until one of them hit him on the shoulder. He stepped back quickly, and the girls disappeared among the coats, with three soft, nasty chuckles.

'Don't be silly,' Charlie said loudly. 'Get out of here!'

He thought that would scare them off, but there was no reaction except another chuckle. And when Peter stepped forward, the conkers whirled again, until one of them cracked him on the head and he cowered back into his corner.

'Oh, for goodness' sake!' Charlie marched down between the coat pegs, and put a hand on the shoulder of the nearest girl.

Immediately, all three of them whirled round, giving him such a shock that he whisked his hand away, seeing grotesque white beards and rosy, swollen cheeks. Three tongues poked out at him, shockingly pink, between the lips of the Father Christmas masks the girls were wearing.

'Don't be silly,' Charlie said again, more severely because he was shaken.

He grabbed at the conkers, but the girls scattered down the cloakroom, giggling behind their masks. When they reached the corridor, one of them turned.

'We were only giving him a taste of his own medicine,' she said, distorting her voice into a nasty, nasal whine, to disguise it. 'Attacking him with conkers—the way he attacked Zoë.'

Before Charlie could respond, they were running off down the corridor. He stared after them. He didn't know who had spoken to him, though he thought it might have been Eleanor Martin, but he recognized the one ahead of her. Zoë had run in that heavy, lumbering way ever since she was three.

He looked back down the cloakroom. Peter was still crouching in the corner with his face down, arms wrapped round his head.

'It's all right,' Charlie said. 'They've gone.'

The small, hunched figure didn't move. Charlie felt like leaving him where he was, but there was something disturbing about that stillness. He walked closer, and stood over him.

'Peter?'

Peter lifted his head and stared, without blinking.

'Are you OK?' Charlie said.

Still Peter didn't move. Charlie had a strange feeling that he was somewhere else altogether, cut off in a private place where the sounds and the light fell in quite different ways. His eyes were like glass.

'It's all right. You can get up now.'

Charlie knew the sensible thing was to go away and leave him to recover on his own, but he couldn't turn his back on those eyes. Once, when he was only five or six, he had surprised a deer in the woods by Toller's Mill. For an instant, the two of them had been locked together, at opposite ends of a stare, each of them gazing into an alien world. Peter's eyes were like that.

Looking into them, Charlie felt as if he had double vision. He still saw Peter—scrawny and irritating, with a red mark on his forehead where the conker had hit him—but he was also seeing a wild creature. He could hear the light, nervous breathing and feel the terror.

Very slowly, as if he were reassuring a frightened animal, Charlie reached out a hand and let it fall gently on to the tense, trembling shoulder in front of him.

And Peter turned his head and bit it. Hard.

'You little—!'

Charlie jumped back, nursing his fingers, and Peter bolted, staggering up the cloakroom so fast that he threw himself off balance. The soles of his shoes scrabbled at the ground, like claws.

'What was that for?' Charlie yelled. 'I was only trying to help.'

He didn't expect a reply. The shout was just to relieve his own feeling of stupidity. But Peter caught at the coats to slow himself down and stopped, with the length of the cloakroom between them.

'I . . . didn't mean . . . ' His voice was hoarse and rusty. 'It was like a trap.'

Charlie drew a long, shaky breath. 'Yes,' he said, when he could speak easily. 'Yes, I know.'

'You were . . . kind.' Peter cleared his throat. 'And that other time. With the photograph. I never said—' He looked awkward and wretched, standing with his weight on one foot.

'You don't have to be grateful,' Charlie said. 'Just don't bite me next time. OK?'

He smiled, to show that it was a joke, and something that was almost a smile flickered across Peter's face. Then he bolted again, running off towards the playground.

Charlie looked down at his hand. There were tooth marks clear across all four fingers. Livid dents that hurt when he flexed his knuckles. He looked down at them and thought about being afraid. So afraid that you defended yourself with your teeth. He wondered what it would be like to walk

66

warily all the time, waiting for a blow, or an attack. Alert for enemies behind the coat pegs.

Paralysed with terror when your father snapped at you.

It was another world. Remote.

The bell rang, sudden and tinny, and he started walking towards his next lesson. In a few seconds he was surrounded by people, laughing and shoving, but they felt strange and distant. When they brushed against him, he could feel the chill from their coats, but their voices seemed like senseless noise.

Swinging away from them, into the history room, he sat down at the back, next to the window, pulling his books out of his bag. The warm air rose stale and stuffy from the radiator beside him and he felt suffocated.

Then he looked up, and the light through the window hit him like a blow in the face.

There was a strong wind blowing, and everything on the other side of the window was alive with movement. Real and bright as the skin on his fingers, and the marks of Peter's teeth. Holly berries flamed scarlet. Cobwebs hung from the dancing bushes like sculptures of spun steel. A lingering elder leaf flapped, acid-yellow, over the stripped stalks of a cluster of berries. It was the same view that he saw every history lesson, but it was utterly changed. Vivid and joyful.

Double vision.

His eyes focused on tiny details, and he felt his brain open to take in the vast brightness. The wild intricacy of it all.

From somewhere far away, a foggy blur of sound forced itself into his ears. 'Willcox!'

It was an effort to look round. He made himself turn his head, and found that he was facing Mr Jarvis's angry stare.

'Are you with us, Willcox?'

67

'Sir . . . ' Charlie began. His own voice sounded thin and distant. He blinked, trying to pull his mind back into the room, and concentrate on the lesson.

Mr Jarvis's frown vanished. 'Are you ill? You look dreadful.'

'Everything's . . . different.' Charlie rubbed a hand across his eyes. 'Strange.'

'Sounds like a migraine to me. Do you want to see the nurse?'

'All right,' Charlie said. 'Thank you, sir.'

He stood up and walked to the door in a sort of daze, but he had no intention of going to the nurse. He felt perfectly all right—except that he was seeing the world in a different way. And he knew just what he wanted to do about it.

He walked straight out of school and went home to collect his cameras. At midday, he was down by the river, where the railway crossed it at Sharps Bend.

By four o'clock, he had taken two rolls of colour film and one of black and white. Strange, precise shots, not like anything he'd done before. The thick, ribbed bark of the willow trees. The empty, spreading seed heads of the cow parsley. The dark arch of the railway bridge, with ferns dripping from its underside.

Images from another world.

Chapter Eleven

Charlie's friends didn't notice the change. They'd always teased him about taking photographs, but they weren't remotely interested in any pictures, except shots of themselves, pulling funny faces.

Zoë noticed though. And she didn't like it.

She came round one day while Charlie was showing his mother some of the new river pictures, and she narrowed her eyes at them. And a couple of weeks later they met in the trees behind Kenworthy's, and he asked her to leave him alone, because her chattering was spoiling his concentration. As she went, she gave him a very strange look.

But she didn't make any comments. Not then. She went on watching and frowning, and he could feel the disapproval boiling up inside her, but she kept it to herself.

Until Christmas Day.

They were all at Alison's house, sitting round the table pulling crackers. *You're lucky to have a big family Christmas,* Charlie's mother always said. *Most only children would give their eye teeth for the kind of time you have.*

Zoë tugged at her cracker and pulled out the paper hat. Settling it on her hair, she gave Charlie a challenging look.

'Well?'

'Well what?' Charlie said.

'Well, what about taking a picture of me?' Zoë leaned across the table. 'Or are you too *artistic* for that sort of thing now?'

Charlie stared at her. Her face was flushed and her hat was a particularly ugly shade of purple. For one second, he thought how horrible he could make her look if he photographed her with a blue filter.

'Don't be silly,' he said. 'I don't know what you mean.'

Zoë scowled at him. 'You never take any nice pictures now. Not pictures of people.'

'Yes I do.'

'No you don't. It's all trees and weeds. And you keep drifting round and *staring*. As if you were under a spell or something.'

Charlie knew she was right, but it was difficult to explain why he didn't want to take Jolly Family Snaps, so he did his best. He took the same pictures as he'd taken last year. And the year before. And the year before that.

Everyone in paper hats.

Zoë with a huge plate of turkey in front of her.

Rachel unwrapping her jodhpur boots. (It had been a Walkman last year.)

Uncle Bill snoring.

It was very hard work, because it was boring. He kept smiling, to disguise how he felt, but he could see that Zoë knew. She started clowning around and demanding to be photographed, almost as if she meant to provoke him.

He finally cracked at nine o'clock, when she changed into her new leggings and started crawling around the floor.

'Come on, Charlie. Take a picture of me being a pony. And Rachel in her new boots.'

She began cavorting about, whinnying and nuzzling Rachel's hand. Rachel was laughing helplessly, but Charlie couldn't stand it.

'I think I'll go for a walk,' he said.

'A walk?' Zoë's eyes widened. 'You can't. We're just going to have supper, and cut the cake.'

But Charlie had already taken the ritual photograph of the Beautiful Christmas Cake. He ignored Zoë and slipped over to Alison.

'Do you mind if I go out for a bit? I'm longing to try out my new flash gun. And those filters you gave me.'

Alison looked across at Charlie's mother and then waved a hand. 'Why not? Get a bit of fresh air.'

'Take a torch,' Charlie's father murmured. 'And watch out for drunks.'

Charlie grinned and nodded, half-way through the door. He heard Zoë call out behind him—'I'll come with you!'—but he ignored her. Two minutes later, he was walking down the road, with the torch in his pocket and his bag over his shoulder.

What was he going to do? It was Christmas Day, and he was out there in the dark, with a fresh roll of film and a new flash gun. That called for something special.

The otter . . .

The moment the idea came into his head, he knew that nothing else would do. Tonight was the night. He was sure of it. With long, straight strides, he struck off down Lammas Hill, towards the old town.

Up on the hill, outside the tight curve of the river, the streets were quiet. People were shut up in their own houses, behind thick hedges and thickets of trees, and Charlie was the only person out walking. Once or twice, he thought he heard a footstep behind him, but when he turned to look, there was no one there.

Ahead, at the bottom of the hill, were the lights of River Walk. Looking down the slope, Charlie could see the strip of darkness behind them, where the secret, unlit river flowed, but as he got lower the houses loomed tall and the river disappeared. He was surrounded by windows full of Christmas trees, and dazzled by the headlamps of passing cars.

Even the Luttrells' house was bright. Walking towards it, Charlie could see a yellow beam shining across the garden and as he drew level, he glanced sideways, looking through the gap between the curtains.

They were watching the television. And something had happened. He could see it, just by looking at them. Jennifer and Mrs Luttrell were sitting on the edge of the sofa, darting quick, nervous glances at Mr Luttrell. And he was very still and upright in an armchair, staring at the screen, almost without blinking. His lips were clamped together and his face was very pale.

There was no sign of Peter.

A small, uneasy shiver ran down the back of Charlie's neck. He couldn't see any other lights in the house, and he didn't want to think of Peter on his own, in the dark.

He loitered for a moment, waiting for the door of the room to open and Peter to sidle in. It didn't happen. The Luttrells stayed just as they were, fixed in their spiky tableau.

But from further along the road, there was a sudden, drunken shout. *Where are you, Jackson? We're coming to get you!* Charlie was suddenly aware that he was carrying both his cameras. An expensive bagful of breakable equipment. Hurrying on, he slipped round the corner, into the entrance of the alley.

He thought he would be out of sight there, but, almost at once, there was an answering shout from the far end of the alley. *Just you try!* Then a giggle, and the sound of people slithering around on the river bank.

He was caught in the middle, and it wasn't a sensible place to be. The first gang was getting closer. Any second now, they would turn down the alley, and there would be a fight. Charlie looked round for somewhere better to hide.

There was only one possible place. He would have to step over the low wall of the Luttrells' front garden and slip through the side gate, into the darkness at the back. He would be completely hidden there, and he could wait out of sight until the coast was clear.

He took the low wall in a stride and put his hand on the wrought-iron gate latch, lifting it carefully, so that it didn't rattle. Then he stepped through, into the shadowy garden, closing the gate softly behind him. He had a vague memory of seeing a dustbin somewhere behind the gate, so he took out Alison's torch and flashed it round quickly. He didn't want to give himself away by crashing against the bin.

He only meant to turn it on for a second, while he had a quick glance round, but when the light found the dustbin he saw something that made him hold the torch steady. Staring.

The dustbin was full of parcels wrapped in Christmas paper, crammed in so that the lid wouldn't shut. Unopened parcels.

For a moment, Charlie thought he must have made a mistake, and that the boxes were empty already. But when he went closer, he saw a small tear in the paper of the top parcel. Inside was a book with a shiny paper jacket, and he could see the letters on the spine. *Every Boy's Handbook.*

There was only one boy in that house.

Charlie moved so that his body shielded the torch. Then, as the two gangs clashed noisily in the alley outside, he lifted off the dustbin lid and moved the top parcel. The one below had a gift tag lying on top. *To Peter from Jennifer.* The wrapping paper was smooth and untorn and the parcel, when he prodded it, was solid inside. A box of something.

Very softly, he laid the dustbin lid on the ground and lifted out the other parcels. There were five of them altogether. All addressed to Peter, and all unopened. It had to be a mistake.

But who would make a mistake like that?

Charlie put the parcels back, trying to remember exactly how they had been lying, as if someone might come out and check their precise positions. Then he put the dustbin lid on top of the heap.

He couldn't imagine what kind of row would end up with a child's Christmas presents in the dustbin, but images seethed in his mind. Mr Luttrell's expression when the tea splashed over his trousers. Peter's face, as he slid away into the garden. And the scene in the sitting room, with three of them sitting watching the television while Peter was—

Where?

Maybe he was in bed, but it was only half past nine. When Charlie shone his torch up at the bedroom windows, he saw that all the curtains were still open.

His heart thudded, and he turned to shine the torch down the garden. The brown wooden shed by the back gate was just as he remembered. Squat and dark, with one window and the door padlocked shut. He could even see the key in the padlock.

The idea in his head was so dreadful that he knew he should test it. He ought to walk to the shed and shine his torch through the window. It would only take a few steps, and there wouldn't be anything there. Except a lawnmower, maybe, and some flower pots. One look would get rid of what he was thinking.

But he couldn't do it.

Instead, he found himself walking back through the side gate, into the front garden. The two gangs were still in the alley, yelling insults at each other, but he ignored that. Stepping over the wall, he ploughed past them and walked out into the street, turning left to head back to Alison's.

And a hand shot out of a hedge and grabbed him.

He almost fainted. Then a voice hissed out of the shadows. 'Where have you been? What were you doing in *that* garden?'

It was Zoë. He dragged her into the light and shook her. 'What are *you* doing, wandering round on your own? You must be mad.'

'I wasn't meant to be on my own,' Zoë said bitterly. 'I was going to catch you up when you took a camera out of your bag. So you could take pictures of me with your new flash.' She scowled. 'You used to like taking pictures of me. Before you changed.'

'I haven't changed.'

'Oh yes, you have!' Her voice rose. 'Or why would you walk out on us—on *Christmas Day*—and go to visit him?' Her hand shot out, pointing back at the Luttrells' house. 'I know who lives there. And he's done something weird to you. That's why you're different.'

'Don't be silly,' Charlie said. 'You're talking rubbish because you're tired. Let's go back and I'll take a photo of you eating a huge piece of cake. Even bigger than last year's.'

She grunted and fell into step with him as he started to walk back up to Alison's. But he had a nasty feeling that he hadn't made her change her mind.

Chapter Twelve

He was right.

For the rest of the holiday, he hardly saw her, because he spent every minute down by the river, photographing the cold details of the year's end. Brittle, frosty leaves. Black birch twigs, shivering and bare. Reeds frozen into ice in the shallow backwaters.

But on the first Friday of the new term, he was packing his bag at the end of the day when Rachel appeared in his tutor room. She stood in the doorway, looking uncertainly at him.

Charlie grinned. 'Hi, Raz. Looking for me?'

'Sort of,' Rachel said. She drifted over to his desk and muttered nervously. 'It's . . . Zoë. She's down in the gym. I think she's going to get into terrible trouble.'

'What's she up to?' Charlie could see Keith waiting for him, and he didn't want to waste time rescuing Zoë. She was tough enough to look after herself.

'I can't say.' Rachel looked nervously round the room. 'I think you ought to come and see. It's Peter—'

'Peter?'

Charlie's voice was too loud. Jennifer lifted her head at the back of the room and took a step towards him, but he didn't wait for her. He picked up his bag and headed for the door.

There was no noise coming from the gyms, but when he pushed the first door open, he saw Zoë and Eleanor over on the far side. They had Peter backed up against the wall bars.

'You don't like it, do you?' Zoë was hissing. 'It makes you shudder.'

As she spoke, she pushed her hand at Peter. At first, Charlie thought she was threatening him with her fist and then he saw that her fingers were clenched tightly round some small object. That was what she kept thrusting into his face, and when he turned his head away, she grinned, triumphantly.

'You see! You can't bear it. And you know what that means.'

Peter's face twisted, and his mouth opened, as if he were struggling to speak.

'Shut up!' Zoë said. Her hand darted forward and she pushed the thing she was holding right into Peter's mouth, jamming it in. His face twisted, and he gagged, but he couldn't take it out, because Zoë and Eleanor seized his arms, twisting them up behind his back.

'What's going on?' Charlie pushed the door wide open and strode towards them. 'Do you want him to throw up?'

Zoë spun round. 'What are you doing here?'

Charlie ignored her and reached for the thing in Peter's mouth. He had assumed that it was some kind of small ball, like a golf ball, but as he touched it, he realized what it was.

A whole bulb of garlic.

'What's this?' he said, staring down at it.

Zoë looked sulky and defensive. 'None of your business. What are you doing here, anyway?'

Charlie glanced back at the door, but Rachel had disappeared. He couldn't blame her. Zoë would give her a hard time if she knew.

'Maybe he was *summoned*,' Eleanor said. Her voice was oily with unspoken suggestions.

'Don't be ridiculous!' Charlie caught hold of Peter's sleeve, pulling him free of their hands. Then he thrust the garlic at Zoë. 'You can have this. Since you're so fond of it.'

Zoë took it, with a scornful lift of her head. 'I haven't got any reason to be frightened of garlic.'

Suddenly, Charlie realized what was going on. He looked at Zoë, incredulously. 'You think Peter's a vampire?'

'Of course I don't!' Zoë snapped. 'I don't believe in vampires.'

Charlie looked at her. 'So what do you believe?'

'Well, if you must know—'

Zoë was defiant, but Eleanor put a quick hand on her arm.

'Don't tell *him*. Remember how he turned up out of nowhere, just when Peter needed him? You mustn't trust him.'

Zoë's expression changed. 'Let's get out of here.'

Shoulder to shoulder, the two of them marched across the gym. As they reached the door, Charlie turned and called after them.

'Next time you want to dabble in superstition, try and get it right. Garlic's for vampires. Maybe you ought to read it up in the library.'

Zoë tossed her head and pulled open the door of the gym. She found herself face to face with Jennifer, who was standing just outside the door. For a second there was a frosty, unpleasant silence. Then Zoë turned and spat two words at Charlie.

'More summoning!'

She and Eleanor pushed their way out and disappeared, and Jennifer walked in, looking puzzled and apprehensive.

'What's up?'

'Silly games.' Charlie grinned drily. 'I hope they *do* go to the library and ask for books about black magic. Mrs Ramm will soon sort them out. She hates all that stuff.'

'Black magic?' Jennifer said. She looked at Peter. 'What have you been doing?'

Until that moment, he hadn't moved, and now he just shrugged, without saying a word. His face was white and shaken.

'I don't suppose he's been doing anything,' Charlie said, for him. He turned to Peter. 'You mustn't put up with that sort of thing. Let me know if they try it on again. I know what Zoë's like.'

Peter ducked his head. 'Thanks.' He began to edge away, towards the door of the gym.

'Clean your teeth when you get home,' Jennifer said sharply. 'You stink of garlic. And you know what Dad's like.'

Peter shot her one long, incomprehensible look. Then he bolted, scuttling away through the door.

'Your dad won't really make a fuss, will he?' Charlie said, when the door closed. 'Not if he knows Peter was being bullied?'

Jennifer's mouth pinched tight. 'Peter ought to have more sense. He knows Dad's under a lot of pressure.'

'What's that got to do with anything?'

'You wait until *your* mother goes senile,' Jennifer said bitterly. She ran a slow hand along the wallbars. 'Gran's too old to look after herself, but she won't come and live with us. She keeps wandering off, and getting into a terrible state and Dad has to go and sort her out. And then she yells and blames *him*, as if he was six or something. And he hates mess. He—' She broke off and looked away. 'He was just about managing until that thing started coming into the garden. That was the last straw.'

Charlie wanted to be sympathetic, but he couldn't stop his heart leaping with excitement. 'That animal's still around?'

'Every night now. Dad goes round the garden before breakfast, looking for tracks.'

'And . . . the poison?'

Jennifer pulled a face. 'That was useless. It wouldn't touch it. It was as if it *knew*.'

'And he still thinks it's rats?'

'Yes . . . but I'm sure he's wrong! I wish I could prove it. He might stop going on about it then.'

Charlie looked down at his fingernails. 'A photograph would be proof.'

'I can't see how to get one.' Jennifer frowned. 'You said I needed an automatic switch, but I've asked at Wilson's and everything like that costs a fortune.'

'You could make one.' Somewhere at the back of Charlie's brain, there was a little shiver of excitement. 'Something simple and mechanical.'

Jennifer looked doubtful. 'Such as?'

'Something that the thing will trip when it treads on a board, or knocks against a lever.' Charlie pushed the door open and led the way out of the gym. 'It wouldn't need to be very complicated. Just something we could hide near the place where it gets in.'

'Maybe,' Jennifer said slowly. 'But it can't be anything that messes up the garden. Dad would go mad.'

'No need for that.' Charlie was on the verge of pulling out his notebooks and sketching a couple of possibilities. But something stopped him.

He didn't want Jennifer to go off and build the switch on her own. He wanted a share in it. And he wanted some of the pictures too, for his photo essay.

'Let me think about it,' he said carefully. 'I'm quite good at things like that. I bet I can work out a way to do it.'

'You won't tell anyone?'

'I won't tell a soul.' He gave her a reassuring grin. 'I'm quite good at keeping secrets, too.'

Fleetingly, Jennifer smiled back. Almost as if she trusted him.

Chapter Thirteen

He thought it would be easy to put some kind of automatic switch together, but he was wrong. It wasn't that he didn't have any ideas. He had plenty of good ideas, and he built four different prototypes involving levers and loops of wire. Two of them even worked, sometimes.

But sometimes wasn't good enough. There might not be more than one chance to get a picture, so the switch had to work reliably, every time. But it had to reset itself too, in case it got tripped accidentally, by some other animal. None of his switches did everything right. One of them broke, and one of them stuck, and the other two were temperamental and unpredictable. By the end of February, Charlie was getting sick of the whole thing.

He sat on his bed on a Sunday morning and looked at his latest contraption in disgust. It worked brilliantly—except that it always got in the way of the lens, so that the beautiful pictures it took were all of its own wires and levers.

'Nothing clever about taking self portraits,' he said out loud. 'Any fool with a cable release can do that.' He glared at it.

And then he heard what he'd said. *A cable release.* Just a cable connected to the camera. With a rubber bulb on the other end, that you squeezed to work the shutter release . . .

That was it! He was the fool! He'd wasted weeks fiddling around with complicated machinery when all he needed was a cable release and a board that would rock when someone trod on it.

By the end of the day, he had those sorted out and ready for the final test. All he had to do now was try the switch out on someone as unsuspecting as the otter would be.

He set it up just inside his bedroom, covered the board with a mat and then opened his door, which had been tightly closed for hours.

'Mum!' he called.

There was a muffled answering shout from the kitchen. Charlie couldn't catch the words, and he called again.

'Can you come up here a minute?'

His mother's voice gargled up the stairs. ' . . . bit busy . . . '

'Please!' Charlie went back into his bedroom, shut the door and waited. That was the best thing to do. Mum was certain to come if she didn't get an answer, just in case it was something serious.

Sure enough, after a moment or two he heard feet on the stairs. Grinning to himself, he sat down on the bed, on the far side of the room, and waited. The door was flung open—

—and the switch worked.

Someone stepped through the door, straight on to one end of the board. It rocked like a seesaw, thumping down on to the air bulb of the cable release. The flash gun exploded in a burst of light and the Pentax's shutter clicked. For an instant, there was absolute silence, except for the sound of the film winding on.

Then a furious voice said, 'What on earth was that?'

It wasn't his mother at all. It was Zoë. She stepped back, bumping into Rachel, who was close behind her, and landed on the board again, squashing the air bulb flat for a second time.

The whole process repeated itself, perfectly.

Charlie didn't know whether to cheer or groan. He hadn't had a clue that Zoë and Rachel were in the house. They were the last people he wanted mixed up with his switch. He went into attack mode before Zoë could get another word out.

'What are you doing here?'

Zoë rolled her eyes up at the ceiling. 'You called, didn't you?'

'I didn't call *you*.'

'Who did you expect? Did you think your mum would come running? All covered in perm lotion, with one side of her hair in rollers?'

Dimly Charlie remembered his mother muttering something about Alison coming to give her a perm. But he'd been too busy thinking about his switch to take it in properly. He certainly hadn't worked out that his dear little cousins would come along too.

Zoë tossed her head. 'So why did you call? And what was that flash? There's something under this mat, isn't there?'

'It's nothing,' Charlie said quickly. 'The flash was an accident.'

But Rachel had noticed the camera. She knelt down and folded back the mat. 'Look, there's a board.'

She put a hand on the long end of the uneven seesaw and it began to dip again. Bending quickly, Zoë pulled at the cable and brought the air bulb slithering out from under the board. Charlie saw her eyes glint, as she realized how the switch worked.

'You were taking a picture up my skirt! That's disgusting!'

She grabbed for the camera and Charlie was only just in time to snatch it away.

'Don't be daft. Why would I want a picture of your knickers?'

Zoë gave him a dark look. 'I don't know. But it's just the sort of thing you would do. *Now*.'

'Don't start that again,' Charlie said wearily. 'I didn't even know you were here, did I?'

'What were you doing then?'

'I was testing my switch.' It came out smoothly. Half true. 'It's an action switch, for photographing trampolinists as they hit the trampoline. I'm going to enter it for the Young Inventor of the Year Award.'

There was a splutter from Rachel, but Zoë didn't even smile. She snorted and stamped off downstairs, with Rachel close behind.

Charlie shut his door. Firmly. He waited a good half hour, until he heard Alison hustling Zoë and Rachel into the car. Then he zapped down to the cupboard under the stairs, where his darkroom was.

He'd used black and white film on purpose, so that he could see the results straight away. He unloaded the camera and, as he placed the unfinished film into the developer, he was grinning in the dark. He'd never thought he would be so eager to see a picture of Zoë's ankles.

The negatives were perfect. Two sharp pictures, taken at exactly the angle he'd wanted, and focused just right. He took the processed film into the cloakroom to wash while he had his tea.

The moment tea was over, he went into the sitting room, to phone Jennifer and tell her he was ready at last. He was afraid that she might put him off until the next day, because it was already quite dark, but she didn't. She sounded just as keen as he was.

'That's wonderful! Come over now. I'll be waiting for you.'

But it was Peter who opened the door. He stood silently staring at Charlie, drying his hands on the long apron he was wearing.

'Hi,' Charlie said.

Peter nearly smiled. While he was still thinking about it, Jennifer appeared at the top of the stairs. She ran down and pushed Peter out of the way.

'Come in! Where's the switch?'

Peter shrank back, down the long hall, and Charlie opened the bag.

'You can't really see anything from looking at the bits. I need to lay it out somewhere.' He looked round the spotless, cream-carpeted hall. That was certainly not the right place.

'Come in here.' Jennifer pushed the sitting room door open. 'Mum and Dad have gone round to Gran's, so we can spread it on the floor. And when I've seen how it works, we'll set it up. Then we can get a picture of the animal if it comes tonight.'

Charlie had never heard her sound so excited. As she hustled him into the sitting room, he was aware that Peter had stopped half-way down the hall, with his back to them. His head was turned slightly, as if to catch what they were saying, but he didn't follow.

Jennifer was kneeling on the floor. 'Hurry up. Let's see.'

Charlie pulled the board out of his bag. 'Have you got any idea where it ought to go?'

'By the end gate,' Jennifer said, without hesitating. 'The one that leads out to the river bank. The footprints are always down at that end of the garden, so it must come in that way.' She leaned forward eagerly. 'What happens? Does it have to tread on the board?'

Charlie nodded. 'On this long end, that's just off the ground. See? That squashes the air bulb from the cable release. Then the elastic pulls the short end down again and resets it.'

Jennifer nodded slowly, taking it in. 'It's very clever. I'm sure—'

Suddenly her head flicked round, towards the door. Charlie turned too. The door was open a crack, and Peter was standing in the gap, peering through at them. The moment they saw him, he scurried off down the hall, and Jennifer jumped up and called after him.

'You're silly. If you're not careful, they'll be back before you've finished the washing up. And you know what Dad's like when he's been to see Gran.'

It wasn't a threat. She sounded almost worried. Charlie laughed awkwardly.

'You're lucky there are two of you. I have to do all the washing up in our house. There's no one to take turns with me.'

Jennifer looked down. 'I wish I *did* do all the washing up,' she muttered. 'It would be much simpler.' She picked up the board, before Charlie could ask what she meant. 'Let's set this up now. Before Mum and Dad get back.'

She led the way down the hall to the kitchen. Peter was standing at the sink, working his way through a pile of washing up. He was up to the elbows in water, scrubbing hard at a saucepan.

Jennifer ignored him. Opening the cupboard by the back door, she took out a torch and pulled on an old jacket. 'We'll have to check that the camera's hidden properly. If the animal sees strange things around, it might look for a different way in.'

'It won't see anything,' Charlie said confidently.

He followed her out, down the garden to the back wall. The shed loomed solid and shadowy at the far end, and

Charlie turned his eyes away as he passed the window. Kneeling down by the gate, he blew on his fingers.

'We'd better do it fast, before we get frostbite. Let's hope the weather doesn't put the animal off.'

He collapsed his tripod as low as it would go and measured the height with his eye.

'This ought to fit under the laurel bush, even with the camera on top. I'll stretch a piece of black polythene among the branches, in case it rains.'

'You'd better fix it tight,' Jennifer said quickly. 'Dad won't like it if there's black polythene blowing round the garden.'

'He won't even see it until the morning.'

Charlie was right. Once the polythene was in place, it was virtually invisible, even when he shone the torch straight at it. Sliding the camera under its shelter, he fixed the flash gun on the far side, wedging it into the bush.

Then he connected up the cable release and laid the air bulb in place on the ground, with the long end of the board poised over it. Anchoring the elastic at the short end to the seven pound weight he'd borrowed from his mother's scales, he gave the whole thing an approving nod.

'It looks just like another paving slab in this light, doesn't it? Shall I test it?'

'I don't think—' Jennifer began.

But Charlie didn't take any notice. He turned off the torch and then stretched out a foot and tapped the board. The flash gun fired, lighting up the end of the garden, and Charlie turned to grin at Jennifer.

As he did so, he saw another shape behind her. Just for an instant, there was a shadowy figure peering round the corner of the shed. Then it ducked away, into the darkness. Charlie knew who it was, and he opened his mouth to call out.

At that moment, there was the sound of a car drawing up in front of the house. It sounded very loud in the crisp, cold air. The engine died, and two doors slammed. Charlie shut his mouth again. Better not to make trouble.

'That's Mum and Dad,' Jennifer said quickly. 'Do you want . . . ?'

She looked nervously at the back gate and then over her shoulder, at the house. Charlie got the message.

'I'll go out this way. Your mum and dad won't want to be bothered with me.'

Jennifer gave him a small, grateful smile and reached across the board to unlatch the gate. 'Don't set the flash off again.'

Charlie grinned. With one stride, he stepped over the board and out of the garden, on to the river bank. He waved his bag at Jennifer. 'I hope you get some pictures tonight. See you at school tomorrow.'

Jennifer nodded and gave him a little wave as he pushed the gate shut. He was just about to walk away when he heard the kitchen door open. Mrs Luttrell called softly down the garden.

'Jennifer? Peter?'

'Coming!' Jennifer called back. She began to walk up the path.

There was no answer from Peter, but Charlie could hear feet tiptoeing quietly across the grass, hurrying towards the house. They were half-way there when Mr Luttrell shouted in a sharp, impatient voice. 'Peter! Where are you?'

'It's all right.' That was Mrs Luttrell, fluttering and anxious. 'He's just popped out into the garden—'

'In the middle of washing up?' Mr Luttrell's voice rose. 'Come here, boy!'

Slowly, the footsteps trailed up to the kitchen door.

'Don't!' Mrs Luttrell said breathlessly.

Mr Luttrell ignored her. 'Haven't you got any *sense*, you stupid boy? There are *rats* out there. Were you going to come straight in and start drying the plates? That we eat off? Don't you understand—'

Charlie froze, expecting a tirade. An explosion. But the voice stopped, and footsteps came back down the garden. One pair with hard shoes that clumped heavily on the path, and another, lighter pair that dragged. When they were almost at the gate, a wooden door creaked, and there was a small, metallic click. Like the click of a padlock.

The heavy feet went back up the garden on their own, and the kitchen door closed again.

Charlie stood very still, with his heart thudding, thinking how easy it would be to walk back through the gate and unlock the shed door. Except that he was too frightened to do it.

He walked slowly away along the river bank, feeling shaken and unhappy. He hoped the switch was going to work and give Jennifer her photographs.

He hoped she was right to think they would make a difference.

Chapter Fourteen

He thought he would see Jennifer the next day, and find out what had happened. But in the night it snowed heavily and, by morning, all the schools were closed. Charlie had no time to think about photography. He spent the day helping his father clear the pavement, so that old Mrs Jeavons next door could walk to the corner shop.

Then it snowed again. And again. By Wednesday morning, the snow was thicker than ever. Mr Willcox looked through the window at breakfast and pulled a face.

'We'll have to clear the path all over again.'

'Don't be such a grouch,' Charlie's mother said. She was gleeful. 'That won't take a minute. And after lunch we can all go over to Alison's and build an igloo. I've always promised Zoë that we'd do that next time there was enough snow.'

'Great!' Charlie said.

His father grinned. 'You haven't shovelled enough snow already?'

'An igloo's different.'

'Of course it is,' Mrs Willcox whisked the porridge plates away and stood up. 'Stop moaning, Grumpy, and get out on the pavement.'

By two o'clock, they'd cleared the path and had lunch. They were just wrapping themselves up in lots of warm layers when the telephone rang. Charlie went to answer it, wearing so many pairs of gloves that he could hardly lift the receiver.

'Yes?'

It was Jennifer. 'I got some!' she said, without any introduction. 'I'm just off to collect them.'

'Off to collect what?' Charlie's mind was full of igloos, and for a moment he couldn't think what she was talking about.

'The pictures. I'm going down to the chemist's now.'

Suddenly, Charlie was there. 'The switch worked?'

'Well . . . yes.' Jennifer hesitated.

'Something went wrong?'

'Not exactly, but—' Jennifer gulped. 'Something . . . chewed through the elastic.'

'*Chewed through it?*'

'I think so. The broken bits of elastic are ragged, and there were tracks all round that end of the board. It's . . . not a cat or anything.'

'It's all right,' Charlie said gently. 'It's not going to be a rat.'

'Oh, I hope not!'

'Can I come and see the pictures?'

'You can meet me at the chemist's. If you like.' Jennifer sounded carefully offhand. So offhand that Charlie knew that was why she had phoned. And he didn't need persuading.

'OK. But don't wait. Start coming back and I'll meet you on the way home.'

He put the phone down and went out into the hall.

'I've got to go over to Jennifer Luttrell's for a bit.'

His mother looked horrified. 'But what about the igloo? Zoë and Rachel will be furious if you don't come.'

'I've got to do this first,' Charlie said stubbornly.

His mother would have gone on arguing, but Mr Willcox put a hand on her arm. 'Let the lad do what he's got to. We'll manage fine on our own.'

She gave up then, but she was still disappointed. 'You'll come down later on, won't you?'

'Of course,' Charlie said. 'I've got to collect one of my cameras from Jennifer's. I'll bring it down with me and immortalize the igloo.'

He knew that would cheer her up, and it did. She grinned. 'I hope you'll do some digging too!'

Charlie nodded. He didn't see that he would need to be long at Jennifer's. He waved them off, and gave Jennifer half an hour to get to the chemist's. Then he slung his camera bag over his shoulder and began walking.

He timed it just right. When he reached Kenworthy's, he could see her coming down the High Street and they met at the Old Bridge.

'Well?' Charlie said.

Jennifer gave a little, embarrassed laugh. 'Actually . . . I haven't looked at them yet. Just in case—' She went suddenly pink. 'I suppose you think that's stupid.'

'No,' Charlie said. 'It's not stupid. But you don't need to worry.' He held out a hand. 'Want me to look first?'

She nodded and passed him the yellow envelope. 'Let's just get round the corner. Out of the wind.'

They crossed the bridge and went round into River Walk. Once they were in the shelter of the houses, Charlie stopped and opened the envelope.

There was a note from the developers saying that most of the film was blank. He slid the prints out, without reading it properly, and looked down at the top one.

It was a picture of his own foot on the board, sharply lit by the flash. The picture he'd taken when he was testing the switch. He shuffled it to the back.

The picture underneath was not such a good shot, but it was clear enough. The otter's round head was just lifted from the ground, caught in a pool of flash light. Its profile stood out sharp against the snow, whiskers fountaining from the muzzle. It was standing in the garden looking towards the gate.

Charlie held it out to Jennifer. 'See? No rats.'

She let out a long, slow breath. 'Thank goodness,' she said. 'But what is it?'

Charlie hesitated. He wasn't ready to stick his neck out yet. 'Let's see if there's a better shot.'

He slipped the picture round to the back—and found himself looking at his own foot again. There were only two prints in the envelope. Frowning, he pulled the negatives out and held them up to the light.

'What happened to the other one?'

'What other one?' Jennifer said. 'What are you doing?'

Charlie slipped everything into the envelope and gave it back to her. 'Think it through. The elastic was holding down the short end of the board. So when it was broken—or chewed—the long end of the board would have come crashing down. Which must have taken a picture. Right?'

'Right.' Jennifer nodded. 'And that's what we've got, isn't it?'

'How did the animal get into the garden then?'

'What do you mean?'

'If that picture was taken when the animal chewed through the elastic, what about when it jumped over the gate? Or did it come in a different way?'

Jennifer shook her head. 'It would have left footprints. The only tracks were between the shed and the gate. It *must* have come over the gate.'

'Then it took that picture when it jumped in. And something else must have broken the elastic.' Charlie had a sudden, sharp memory of a shadowy figure running away from the flash. 'Or *someone* else. Someone who understood the switch and stopped it working.'

'What do you mean?' Jennifer's voice was uneasy.

'Oh, come on! Who else knew about the camera? Who was down there snooping, while we were setting it up?'

'*Peter?*'

'That's right. He must have come back later on and destroyed the switch.'

Jennifer shook her head. 'That's impossible. It wasn't Peter.'

'Then the animal must have been in the garden already,' Charlie said, exasperated. 'How do you explain that?'

'I don't know. I don't care. But it wasn't Peter who broke the elastic.' Jennifer turned and began to walk briskly up the road.

'How can you—?'

How can you be so sure? Charlie was going to say, but he stopped suddenly. Because he was afraid that he knew the answer. Remembering how the padlock had clicked in the dark, he just wanted to walk away and forget all about the Luttrells.

Then he thought of his camera and his flash gun, sitting in their house. He trudged through the snow after Jennifer, and caught her up at the front door.

'All right if I come in and pick up my things?'

'Please yourself.' Jennifer put her key in the lock.

Before she could turn it, her mother opened the door. She blinked at Charlie. 'Oh. Hallo.'

'Hallo,' Charlie said. He wondered what she would offer him this time. Scotch pancakes? Rock buns?

She didn't offer anything. Her eyes slid towards the envelope in Jennifer's hand. 'Photographs?'

'Yes!' Jennifer stepped into the house. Even before Charlie had shut the door behind them, she was opening the envelope. 'I've got a picture of Dad's rat!' she said triumphantly.

Mrs Luttrell leaned forward to peer at the photograph, and Mr Luttrell appeared behind her in the hall.

'What's that about rats?' he said sharply.

Jennifer went towards him with the picture, almost running. 'Look, it's all right! You don't have to worry! It's not rats at all. It's something quite different.'

He almost snatched the photograph out of her hand. His face twisted as he looked down at it.

'It's not a rat,' Jennifer said again. Sounding as hasty and anxious as her mother. 'You don't need to worry—'

'No, it's not a rat,' Mr Luttrell said.

Jennifer stopped dead. His voice was thick with disgust. For a moment, they were all looking at him, waiting, and even Charlie found himself holding his breath.

'What is it?' Mrs Luttrell whispered.

'Filthy little mink.' Suddenly Mr Luttrell's hand clenched, screwing the picture into a crumpled ball. 'I'm not having *those* moving into the garden.'

He pushed the ruined photograph back into Jennifer's hand and spun round, marching down the hall towards the kitchen. When he was almost there, Peter came through the kitchen door.

'Out of my way,' Mr Luttrell said impatiently.

He shoved Peter aside, like a piece of furniture, and strode into the kitchen. Mrs Luttrell scuttled after him.

'What shall I do? Phone the Pest Control Officer?'

'No point in wasting your time,' Mr Luttrell said icily. 'He won't be any more use than he was last time. We've got to take proper action ourselves. Before the garden gets infested with droppings. And germs.'

'Maybe there's only one—' Mrs Luttrell murmured.

'You can't let these things slide.' Mr Luttrell opened the back door. 'We've got to keep in control. Unless you want the garden full of mink.'

He went out into the garden, and Peter inched down the hall.

'Mink?' he said softly.

Jennifer smoothed out the crumpled photograph and held it out. When Peter was near enough to see, he stopped very still and stared, without blinking. Without moving at all, except for his restless, twisting fingers.

Charlie looked down at the fingers. And then at the ugly, jagged creases that ran across the otter's face. 'You could get another print made,' he murmured, trying to sound ordinary and matter-of-fact.

'No point, is there?' Jennifer said bitterly. 'I only wanted the picture because I thought it would help. And it's just made things worse.' She glared at Charlie. 'Dad can't help being like that. He just doesn't like . . . germs and things.'

'I know,' Charlie said. 'It's all right.'

But it wasn't all right, and they both knew it. The not-all-rightness stood between them like a barrier.

'I'll get your things,' Jennifer said.

She ran upstairs to fetch them, and Peter followed her. When she came back, he was right behind her, with his coat on.

Mrs Luttrell heard their feet on the stairs and stuck her head out of the kitchen. 'What are you doing?' she said, when she saw Peter. 'You're not going out?'

'I—'

'It's cold out there,' Mrs Luttrell said. 'You'll get wet. And track in slush.'

Peter's eyes flickered towards the door and back, as if he were measuring the distance. He was breathing fast, and there was an odd red flush over his cheekbones.

'I've got to go,' he said roughly.

Mrs Luttrell looked away nervously, towards the back garden. 'It'll only cause trouble.'

'I've *got* to,' Peter said again.

Charlie didn't understand what he meant, but he heard the desperation in his voice. And he knew he'd heard it before. *It was like a trap . . .*

'Can't he come with me, Mrs Luttrell? I need someone to help me with my photographs.'

She blinked, caught off guard, and Charlie gave her his politest, most charming smile.

'It's much too wet to put things down, and that makes it really hard, unless you're a juggler. Can Peter come and hold things for me?'

'*Peter?*'

It sounded fairly improbable to Charlie, too, but he nodded firmly. 'He'd be really useful. Please let him come.' He gave Mrs Luttrell another burst of the PCS.

'You shouldn't trust him to hold anything valuable,' Mrs Luttrell said doubtfully.

'I won't,' Charlie said. 'Thanks for the warning.' He took the bag Jennifer had fetched, avoiding her eyes, and opened the door, pushing Peter through ahead of him. 'I'll bring him back before it's dark.'

He closed the door quickly behind them. Peter was standing still on the path.

'I had to get out,' he muttered. 'But you don't have to—'

The side gate next to them rattled suddenly, and his mouth pinched shut. Mr Luttrell had come up the garden with a piece of chipboard and he was measuring it against the back of the gate.

With a satisfied nod, he lowered it and looked through the black wrought-iron spirals at Charlie and Peter. His eyes were grim and pale. 'That should seal *this* gate off. And I'll put barbed wire across the top of the one at the back. No mink is going to get the better of me.'

Peter drew in his breath. Not loudly, but loud enough for Charlie to hear. Then he turned and walked out of the front garden and down the side alley, towards the river.

Charlie lengthened his stride, to catch up. The snow was thick along the alley, and on top of the wall. 'Where are you going?'

Peter was still one step ahead, marching steadily with his head down and his hands in his pockets. 'Alderpool,' he said.

At least, that was what it sounded like. But it was such a quick mumble, that Charlie couldn't be sure. And anyway, he didn't understand. 'Sorry?'

Peter stopped and turned. The alley was narrow, and the walls stretched back behind him, dark red under their caps of snow. The long lines seemed to focus on his small, upright figure.

'I had to get out,' he said. 'It was like . . . not being able to breathe.'

'Yes,' Charlie said. 'It's all right. I know.'

Peter didn't smile, but his shoulders relaxed, very slightly. 'You ought to go to the alder pool,' he said. 'On past Toller's Mill.' He pointed upstream. 'The snow's good there. You'd get some brilliant pictures. If you really want—' He stopped short and looked nervously at Charlie.

'Show me,' Charlie said.

Chapter Fifteen

The branches of the alders were bare and dark against the snow, and they dangled pale, speckled catkins over the black surface of the river.

Last year, Charlie would have passed the catkins without a second glance. Now, their luminous green made him catch his breath. They shone like candles above the unreflecting water. He moved along the pool, gazing at them from different angles.

Peter watched without saying a word. He simply held out his hand for Charlie's gloves and stood staring as the tripod was set up. Charlie didn't speak either. He was concentrating on the catkins. Working out how to deal with the strong contrast of white snow and black branches without letting it dominate that fragile green.

After twenty minutes or so, Peter said softly, 'If you were on the other bank, you could see the roots.'

'No time.' Charlie blew on his fingers and stamped his feet. 'It's a good twenty minutes' walk to the Old Bridge. And twenty minutes back on the other side. The light would be gone.'

'The bridge?' An odd, puzzled expression flickered in Peter's eyes. Then his face cleared, and he grinned, as though Charlie had said something funny. 'You don't need the bridge. You can cross down there.' He pointed at the reed bed beyond the alder pool. 'If you want to.'

'Cross?' Charlie said. 'In the water?'

'It's not deep.'

Charlie rubbed his hands together and thought how cold the river must be. He was just going to say so, when he realized that he didn't care about that. He did want to see the roots. Peter had been right—more than right—about what a good place the pool was. If the view from the other side matched what he had already seen, he didn't want to miss it. He glanced along the bank, at the tangle of brambles in between them and the reed bed.

'Can't we cross here instead? Where the pool gets narrow?'

It looked simple enough. The black water was clear, in the shadow of the trees. He could see the dapple of pebbles on the bottom.

'Too deep,' Peter said, unhesitatingly. 'You'd have to take off all your clothes.'

He set off towards the brambles and began picking his way through them, so fast that Charlie couldn't believe it. Until he gathered up his things and followed. Then he found that there was a sort of track below the tangle.

It was well hidden. The long brambles looped over it and it ran erratically, twisting left and right for no reason that Charlie could see. But Peter seemed to know just where it was. He lifted his feet high over the loops and, when he trod down, the brambles caved in underneath him, shaking off their snow and pressing flat to the ground.

Charlie started to follow. But he found out, very quickly, that he had to be accurate. Unless he stepped exactly in Peter's dark trail, his feet sank into dense, prickly undergrowth.

'Hey! Wait! I keep losing the path. What is it, anyway? An animal track?'

'Badger,' Peter muttered, watching Charlie disentangle his trousers.

'Are you sure?' Charlie said eagerly, tugging his leg free. 'Have you seen them?'

The only answer was a shrug. Peter had reached the reed bed now, and was kneeling to take off his socks and trainers. He rolled his trousers above his ankles and stepped out confidently into the reeds. A thin, muddy soup oozed between his toes.

'You're sure it's not too deep?' Charlie said.

'You'll be all right in your boots.'

The water was very, very cold. Even through the rubber of his boots, Charlie's feet ached. But he held the camera bag high above his head, and he was across in a couple of minutes, paddling through shallow water on to a little snow-covered beach.

Peter was on the bank above, drying his toes on a handkerchief. On this side, the bank was thick with rusty old nettles, but it was easy to wade through them. They were back at the alder pool in a few seconds.

The moment they reached it, Charlie saw why Peter had told him to cross. The bank where they had been standing before was eaten away by the river. It fell vertically, leaving the tree roots exposed. In any other weather, they would have been barely noticeable, but now the snow had lodged on their narrow ridges, so that they showed up as a complicated, delicate network against the dark bank.

'Hey!' Charlie said. 'That's brilliant!'

Peter laughed suddenly. A high, surprising sound in the cold air. 'I knew you'd like it.'

Charlie didn't answer. He was already setting up his tripod.

* * *

He was hardly aware of anything except the river, until the light began to fail, and Peter tugged at his sleeve.

'I have to go back now. Before they start wondering where I am.'

'What? Oh, yes.' Charlie's concentration broke, and he found himself blinking in the grey, dwindling light. Coming back to his ordinary self, beside the river that he had known all his life.

Except that he realized, now, that he had never known this part at all. He had never noticed the alder catkins. Or the pattern of the tree roots. Or the badger's winding trail, and the squishy shallows of the reed bed.

'Thanks for showing me,' he said. 'This is a special place of yours, isn't it?'

'Sort of.' Peter hesitated. 'Why?'

'No reason,' said Charlie hastily. Not wanting to pry. 'I just thought . . . you know it so well.'

'Not that well.' Peter looked wary. 'No more than anywhere else.'

'You mean—' The words exploded in Charlie's mind, opening the door to a new, unimagined country. 'You mean you know other places this well?'

'Maybe.'

Charlie swallowed and picked up the tripod. For a moment, he actually couldn't remember how it folded. 'Many places?'

Peter shrugged. 'No. Just the river, really. From a bit above here, and all round the town. To the sewage works.'

Charlie thought of the river's long, lazy loop. Four miles of it. He'd measured it on the Ordnance Survey map when he started his essay. Four miles. An idea flamed in his mind, like a sun rising over strange hills.

'Could you . . . tell me about it? I want to know—'

He wanted to know what Peter knew. All of it. Not dragged out in stumbling, awkward sentences, but there instantly, transferred to his own head.

'Could you draw me a *map*? With all that stuff on it?'

The moment the words were out, they sounded ridiculous. Peter shook his head and edged away.

'I can't draw.'

'But the river's easy,' Charlie said. 'Look.'

He squatted down and drew a curve in the snow. Three quarters of a circle, from the south east up to the north and right round to the south west.

Peter frowned. 'What's that?' He was looking at the loop the wrong way up, so that the narrow neck of land in the south was at the top.

'It's the river, of course.' Charlie stood up and moved him round. 'The Old Bridge is here, and this is the New Bridge—'

Peter didn't look any the wiser. Charlie squatted down again, dabbing at the snow.

'This is the alder pool. And Toller's Mill.' He made two little dents with his finger, side by side. 'And here's the Old Bridge, where the loop starts. With River Walk on one side, and Kenworthy's on the other. Then the river gets wider, and here's the New Bridge in the north. Where the road comes down from the motorway—'

Peter's face cleared suddenly. 'Oh yes! And our house is here. Between the alder pool and the Old Bridge.' His finger touched the snow, in exactly the right place. 'I've got it now. It's just that . . . I've never thought of the river like that before.'

'So you'll do the map?' Charlie said.

Peter backed away through the nettles. 'I might,' he said, cautiously. He sat down on the snowy ground beyond the nettles and began to take off his shoes. 'If I do . . . will you take photographs?'

'I might,' Charlie said. He grinned. 'Depends what you've got to tell me about.' He watched Peter slide off the bank and step out into the river. 'Why? Do you want me to?'

Peter stopped and turned back, poised lightly on both feet. Islanded in reeds. Charlie could see his toes, pale under the murky water as the river flowed around and past him. Suddenly he laughed again, the same startling laugh as before.

'It's strange, that picture you gave me. I'd like to see some more.'

He crossed to the other side and scrambled on to the bank. Charlie raised a hand, waving goodbye.

'If you do me the map, I'll give you lots,' he shouted.

Peter pulled on his trainers and set off without answering, and Charlie turned back to his bag, to finish packing up. He thought that was the end of their conversation, but Peter was working his way back through the brambles. When he reached the opposite side of the alder pool, he stopped and called across.

'You know that picture?'

'The one I gave you?' Charlie said. 'With the animal swimming?'

Peter nodded. 'Do you know . . . ' He stopped for a moment. 'What kind of animal do you think it was?'

That wasn't a question about the animal, Charlie thought. It sounded more like a question about *him*. About what was going on in his head.

'I think it was an otter,' he said truthfully. He hesitated, and then went on, because Peter was staring at him. 'I think it was the otter that comes into your garden.'

Peter didn't say anything.

Charlie laughed, awkwardly. 'My father says that's impossible. He says there aren't any otters in this river. What do you think?'

It was getting dark under the alder. Peter's face was shadowed and withdrawn. He waited a very long time before he answered, and when he did, every word was careful and precise.

'I've never *seen* an otter.'

Then he was off, running sure-footedly along the bank.

It was virtually dark by the time Charlie got home. As he stepped through his front door, he heard a familiar voice, and his heart sank.

'I think he's *miserable*. He should have come to help us.'

Zoë. Irate Zoë. Zoë with a grudge. Charlie pulled a face and tried to shut the front door without making any noise. He should have known that it was impossible. At the first, faint sound, Zoë's head appeared round the dining room door.

'Where have you been?'

Rachel's head appeared too, a little lower down. 'You missed the igloo. It was brilliant. Before it fell down.'

'We could have made it stronger,' Zoë said, meaningfully. 'If we'd had another person.'

'Oh, leave the poor boy alone,' Alison called, from inside the dining room. 'Let him come and have some tea. He must be starving.'

'He's probably had tea already.' Zoë's eyes narrowed. 'At Keith's, or somewhere.'

'No, I haven't,' Charlie said. He put his things on the hall table and took off his coat. 'I haven't even seen Keith. I've been down by the river.' Now he was inside, he realized how cold he was. And hungry. He headed for the dining room, but Zoë barred his way.

'You've been on your own? All that time?'

Charlie hesitated. Then he said, 'Oh, nark it, Zoë. Let me in.'

But the hesitation was fatal. He could see her mind buzzing as she stepped back. She looked sideways at Rachel, with a gleeful smile. 'He wasn't on his own, was he? I wonder who she was?'

'It wasn't a she,' Charlie said, losing patience with her. Wanting his tea. 'It was Peter Luttrell, if you must know.'

Zoë's stare sharpened. Silently, she mouthed two words at him. With her back to everyone else. *Evil Eye!*

'Oh, don't be stupid,' Charlie said. He sat down and hacked a thick slice of bread off the loaf.

But he could feel his appetite fading as he cut. There was a cold weight in the pit of his stomach. *He* was the stupid one. He'd just given Zoë another grudge to pile up against Peter.

He looked up at her and smiled, apologetically. Trying to patch things up. 'I'm sorry I missed the igloo. I'll come round tomorrow morning, and we can make another one.'

'No we can't,' Zoë said, bitterly. 'It's going to thaw in the night, and we'll all be back at school tomorrow.'

Chapter Sixteen

She was right. In the morning, the world dripped depressingly. And the local radio was depressing as well.

. . . all schools are open this morning except for Lamington Junior School, where the heating is broken. Pupils from there should listen . . .

Lucky Lamington Juniors, thought Charlie, trudging through slush to the school gates.

It was half-way through the afternoon when Mrs Ramm sent the message to Jennifer. Simon Bradley pushed his head round the door, just as Mr Feinstein was winding up a geography lesson.

'Please can Jennifer Luttrell go to the library?'

'Now?' Mr Feinstein frowned. 'It's only fifteen minutes to break.'

'Mrs Ramm said as soon as possible. Urgently.'

Simon ducked out, and Mr Feinstein glowered at Jennifer. 'Next time you get into a row about library books, make sure it's in someone else's lesson.'

Jennifer bobbed her head apologetically. As she stood up, her face was puzzled and anxious. For a moment, Charlie wondered why. Then he realized how odd it was for Mrs Ramm to interrupt a lesson like that. She was usually meticulous about being polite.

'Hurry up, then!' Mr Feinstein snapped. 'If you're going.'

Jennifer scurried out at top speed, frowning.

When the bell rang, nobody went after her. Anyone else would have had a gaggle of friends racing to the rescue, but Jennifer was too good at being invisible. Everyone had forgotten her, except Charlie.

He gathered his things and muttered to Keith, 'Got to go and look something up. For my Camera Club project.'

That was all he needed to say. Keith snorted and dived outside, and Charlie was left on his own to walk down to the library.

When he pushed the door open, he thought he'd missed Jennifer. The place was virtually empty. Even Mrs Ramm's desk was unoccupied. He was on the verge of leaving again when he saw a sudden movement, off to the right, behind the glass door of the office. Jennifer whisked past it, holding something white.

Charlie walked over and opened the door. 'Hi. I wondered—'

He was going to make up some excuse about ordering a book, but as soon as he stepped into the little room and saw what was happening, the words deserted him.

Peter was sitting on the far side, hunched into Mrs Ramm's swivel chair. He was swathed in a grey blanket, but that didn't hide his blue, pinched face, or the way his whole body was shaking. He looked as though the frost had crept under his skin and shrivelled the flesh tight against his bones.

Mrs Ramm was standing by the kettle, stirring something in a mug. She looked sharply at Charlie. 'I'm not free just now. Come back later on.'

Her voice was quiet, but it was almost as cold as Peter's face. Normally, Charlie would have backed out, feeling squashed, but not this time. He looked at Jennifer and Peter.

'It's all right,' he said. 'I'm their friend.'

The air warmed, faintly, and Mrs Ramm gave him a curt nod. 'That won't come amiss. See if you can get some sense out of this silly boy, then. Find out why he's been doing Games in soaking wet kit. In *this* weather.'

Jennifer twitched the wet shirt and shorts that she was spreading on the radiator. 'Mr Nicholl shouldn't have kept him out there,' she said abruptly. 'He should have noticed.'

'Peter should have told him,' Mrs Ramm said. 'Even teachers haven't got eyes everywhere.' She pursed her lips and gave the mug a last, fierce stir. Then she handed it to Peter. Quite gently. 'Get that inside you. Then we might get by without sending you to Casualty.'

Peter cupped his hands round the mug and sipped. The tomato soup coloured his top lip raucously orange, making the blue of the bottom one even more startling.

'But what's he doing here?' said Charlie. Baffled.

'Because this is where he came,' Mrs Ramm said shortly. She prodded Jennifer with one finger. 'The soup won't get him warm on its own. Take him on your lap or something. Hug him. That's the best way to raise someone's temperature.'

There was an impatient stiffness about the way she said it. Charlie understood. The really sensible thing would have been for them all to hug Peter. To get as close as they could, and share their body heat, until that terrible blueness changed slowly to a warm, living pink. Charlie's mother would have done it, he knew. She would have hauled Peter on to her lap without a second thought and made the rest of them join in. But he and Mrs Ramm had to watch as Jennifer sat down reluctantly and took Peter on her knees. He huddled there, with his face turned away from hers, sipping at the soup, and she wrapped her arms round his waist like someone wrapping a parcel.

'He needs his proper clothes,' Mrs Ramm said. 'Where will they be?'

Charlie opened the door, glad of a job. 'I'll get them.'

Peter's games bag was easy to find, because it was neatly named. As he unhooked it, Charlie had a horrible, inevitable feeling about what was in there. He pushed his hand in.

He was right. The bag was damp, and the clothes inside were even damper. Not obviously, sopping wet, but clammy and cold. And there was a crumpled note, hastily thrust in on top.

Witches hate water

Feeling sick, Charlie thrust it into his pocket. He was horribly afraid that he recognized the handwriting, but he wasn't going to let himself think about it. He had to concentrate on practical things, like finding Peter some dry clothes. Preferably without making a fuss.

The quickest way would be to sneak them out of lost property. Anything he borrowed from there could go back tomorrow, and no one would be any the wiser. But he would have to hurry. Break was nearly over.

He slipped down the corridor to Mr Feinstein's room. It was empty, and he pulled out the lost property boxes and began to burrow. He was looking for something anonymous and shabby, without a name tape. There were three pairs of trousers in the box and he chose the smallest. Then he pulled out a handful of shirts and sweatshirts.

One of the shirts actually belonged to Peter. *P. Luttrell*, said the name tape in the back of the neck. Grimly, Charlie wondered who had put it there. He hoped Mr Feinstein hadn't noticed.

He bundled it up with a sweatshirt that was about the right size and the least repulsive pair of socks he could find, picked up the trousers and headed back to the library. Mrs Ramm was standing with her back to the door of the office, blocking the little window, but she moved out of the way when he knocked.

Peter was pinker now. He was draining the last dregs of tomato soup and looking round with sharp, flickering eyes. Charlie dumped the bundle of clothes on his lap.

'That's the wrong sweatshirt,' Jennifer said, over Peter's shoulder. 'It's got a stain on it.'

'At least it's dry,' Charlie said. 'His own clothes are wet, like his games kit.' He spun round quickly, to face Peter. 'Who did it? Who was picking on you?'

He said it fast, hoping to surprise the information out of him, but Peter's reactions were even faster. He turned his head away, and his thin body tensed under the blanket.

Mrs Ramm shook her head at him. 'Don't be silly. The people who did it are completely irresponsible. And everyone else in your class must be stupid too. They need a lecture on hypothermia, for one thing. It's your duty to make a fuss.'

'No fuss.'

Jennifer and Peter said it together. An automatic reaction. Peter clammed up again, immediately, but Jennifer went on, before Mrs Ramm could argue.

'If there's a fuss, there'll be letters home. To Mum and Dad.'

She stopped. And what she hadn't said yawned like a deep pit in the middle of the office. Mrs Ramm cleared her throat.

'If I had a child,' she said gruffly, 'I would be appalled to think that something like this could happen without my knowing.'

'But you might not understand that it wasn't your child's fault. Especially . . . ' Jennifer paused, choosing words.

'Especially if you had enough to worry about already.' She lifted her head and looked Mrs Ramm straight in the eye. 'You mustn't tell them.'

It seemed impossible for anyone to say another word without starting an argument. It was Peter who broke the silence.

'I'm fine,' he said suddenly. 'Fine.' He slid off Jennifer's lap and pulled on the trousers that Charlie had brought. Then he dropped the blanket. For a split second, Charlie saw his thin, pale body, with the ribs staring. Then the shirt covered it, and Peter was dragging on the sweatshirt, with the shirt buttons still only half fastened.

When he was almost dressed, he snatched up the socks and his trainers and bolted. Jennifer jumped up as if she were going to follow.

'No,' Mrs Ramm said. 'Leave him alone.'

'But that was rude.' Jennifer looked very pink. 'He should have thanked you.'

'That's not important.' Mrs Ramm turned away and rearranged the games kit on the radiator.

'Of course it's important,' Jennifer said. 'I'm really sorry, Mrs Ramm. I'll get him to come back later on and—'

'You certainly will not!' Mrs Ramm spun round and her pale blue eyes were fierce. 'At least he came to ask me for help. That was hard for him. If you make it even harder, he might not come at all next time.'

'Next time?' Jennifer said.

'There's always a next time,' said Mrs Ramm. 'If you let them get away with it.'

'That's right,' Charlie said. 'They're not going to stop just because you ignore them. You ought to do something. Your *parents* ought to do something.'

Jennifer glared at him. 'Don't interfere. You don't understand.'

'We could try,' Mrs Ramm said.

Jennifer shook her head. 'You'll only make things worse.' She turned away and walked out of the office.

Mrs Ramm looked at Charlie. She didn't say anything, but she raised her eyebrows. Charlie put a hand into his pocket and pulled out the note he'd found in Peter's games bag. She read it, and her face puckered as though she'd eaten something sour.

'That's bad. Do you know who wrote it?'

Charlie hesitated, and she screwed the note up, with a sudden, angry movement.

'That's always the way,' she said harshly. 'You have a good idea who's behind it, but never enough to prove anything.' She frowned. 'Were those two right? About not making a fuss and telling their parents?'

'I think . . . probably,' Charlie said. 'There would be trouble. For Peter.'

'And Peter already has as much trouble as he can cope with.' Mrs Ramm nodded. Then she glanced down at the screwed-up note. 'We can do nothing. But it's uncomfortably like washing our hands.' She lifted her head and looked straight at Charlie. Her face was dry and lined. 'If we keep this to ourselves, we have a responsibility to make sure he's all right. To help him, if he needs it.'

'Yes,' Charlie said. 'Of course.'

But that wasn't enough. She went on staring at him until he committed himself.

'I promise,' he said.

Chapter Seventeen

For almost a month, he worked hard at his promise. He kept an eye on Zoë and Eleanor. He charged into the middle of every crowd at school, and went running to every fight, in case Peter was somewhere in the middle, buried under a heap of bodies.

He even tried to talk to Zoë and Eleanor about what they'd done. But that was useless. Zoë denied it all, red-faced and indignant, and Eleanor slid behind her, hissing into her ear.

'He's your cousin, isn't he? He'd be on your side, if he hadn't been . . . influenced.'

And Zoë's face turned blank and hostile, so that Charlie knew it was no good talking to her any more.

The whole thing festered in his head, making him tense and anxious. It even spoilt the river. Whenever he walked along a wild, tangled stretch, he remembered Peter at the alder pool. Happy and strange. And then he remembered that blue, pinched face.

He started to avoid the wild places and keep to the public piece of river below the castle walls. He photographed bricked-up banks and floating Coke cans, old houses rising sheer from the water, and people sitting in riverside cafés.

And then spring arrived.

It happened quite suddenly, on a Monday morning in the middle of April. On Sunday, it was winter, with dripping trees and a harsh wind scouring the streets. But on Monday morning the sun came out and leaves began to open, spreading a green haze everywhere.

The idea of sitting in school was a torment. Standing in front of the bathroom mirror, tying his tie, Charlie looked out of the window and saw the light dancing on new colours. And he wanted to be out there, looking at them. He wanted to explore the morning.

If he waited until the weekend, he would have missed that first, tentative beginning. Spring happened so *fast*.

As he stepped out of the house, the fresh, live smell drifted towards him from all the gardens around, and he knew that he couldn't miss it. He turned back, to fetch his camera bag, and when he came to the Old Bridge, he didn't walk across, towards the school. He turned right, instead, and walked into the strip of woodland behind Kenworthy's.

He was heading for the ruins of Toller's Mill, in the overgrown patch below the alder pool. As he scrambled over the fallen willows and fought his way through the tangle beyond, he could see that the bare willow branches were bright and alive. The great ash tree that leaned out over the water was covered with black buds, dull as suede, and the pale light danced across bright, crumpled leaves on every bush and every creeping tendril.

The thickets hummed with different colours, each bush showing its own distinct shade of red or purple or yellow. Charlie understood, all over again, why Mr Feinstein kept yelling at them to use their eyes. For a whole hour, he did nothing else, as he clambered over the broken walls of the mill, gazing at the water from every angle.

Then he began trying to photograph what he had seen. To capture the precise, amazing conjunctions of colour and shape and light. By midday, he had finished two rolls of colour film. He loaded a third into the Minolta, but he could feel his concentration slipping. He was exhausted and ravenously hungry, and he knew he ought to take a rest and go and find some food.

But he didn't want to leave the river.

He took off his shoes and socks and sat on the edge, trailing his feet in the cold, rushing water. The river was too cold for swimming and too deep for paddling, but he wriggled his toes among the reeds for almost half an hour.

And then he saw the otter.

It appeared without any warning. One moment, he was sitting alone, with his eyes half closed, listening to the water rushing round the logjam of derelict branches beside him. The next, there was a sound of scrabbling, ten metres along the bank. He opened his eyes and saw a dark shape heave itself out of the water, on to the high, gnarled roots of the ash.

Its wet coat clotted into points and drips hung from its whiskers as it steadied itself, gazing back towards the alder pool. Charlie held his breath, waiting for it to turn and see him there. He had no way of reassuring it. All he could do was keep very still, with his eyes turned slightly aside, so that it didn't meet a direct, frightening stare.

It turned quite slowly, as though it had known all along where he was. And it didn't react as he had expected, by slithering straight back down the bank. Its strange, liquid eyes moved over his face quite calmly, until he looked up and met them.

Wild, wary eyes, poised on the very edge of terror. But not terrified. Glassy and remote.

Slowly and smoothly, Charlie slid a hand sideways, to the nearest camera. The rest of his body was completely still. He didn't look down to check the exposure or even to glance into the viewfinder. He shot blind, relying on his instincts.

The otter stared straight back at him.

When he had taken three pictures, Charlie risked moving, very cautiously. He swivelled slightly, so that he could catch the shape of the otter, full against the water, framed by the drooping branches of a willow. Mr Feinstein's voice was hammering in his head.

Panicking never does any good. Don't blow a good picture by snatching at it. Take your time.

Another two shots, and then the otter dropped on to all fours, looking quizzically at Charlie. Suddenly, it went straight over the bank, head first, sliding down a vertical, muddy track and vanishing in a stream of silvery bubbles.

Charlie knew he'd seen another mudslide like that, but he had no time to chase the memory. The otter's head broke the surface, right in front of him. It shook drops of water from its whiskers, rolled over and dived again. This time, he thought he'd lost it, but it reappeared in the smooth sunny stretch above him, its lifted head dark against the brightness.

For maybe ten minutes, while Charlie followed it with his camera, it swam and dived for no obvious reason. Enjoying itself. Then it surfaced on the far side of the river, with a fish clutched to its chest. Charlie saw its jaws clamp together in a single, killing bite and then it dragged the fish on to the muddy little beach opposite and began to eat, stripping off the flesh with sharp, efficient teeth.

By the time the fish was reduced to a pile of bones and scales, Charlie had used all his new colour film and half the roll of black and white in the Pentax. He dropped his hands into his lap and watched without taking any more pictures as the otter groomed itself and stretched in the sun. It was absorbed in its own movements, but completely alert. Contented and self-sufficient.

The end was as sudden as the beginning had been. Without looking round at Charlie, it slipped smoothly into the water and set off downstream. This time, he knew it wouldn't be coming back. He saw the dark shape of its head dwindling in the distance at the point of the long wake. Picking up his camera bag, he began to pack everything away.

He didn't hurry. What he had was too important to spoil by being careless. He wound off the colour film and dropped it in at the chemist's on the way home. Then he went back and let himself into the empty house, to develop the black and white pictures.

But he didn't start straight away. It was over six hours since he'd eaten anything, and he wasn't going to risk fumbling. He wanted steady hands and good judgement.

He ate a sandwich and drank a glass of milk, and then shut himself in under the stairs and started, making himself keep all the rules. No skimping on time. No peeping. Wait for the contact prints.

He was just hanging up the negatives to dry when the phone rang. To begin with, he ignored it. He never let the phone interrupt him when he was in the darkroom, and this time he wasn't supposed to be there anyway.

But whoever was ringing wouldn't give up. The phone went on until it cut out, and then started again, with barely enough of a pause for redialling. In the end, Charlie couldn't bear it any longer. He finished wiping down the negatives and went to answer it.

'Are you all right?' said Rachel's voice. Rather shrill and tense.

'I've got a high fever,' Charlie said pleasantly. 'And three broken legs.' He liked making Rachel giggle.

But she didn't giggle this time. She just caught her breath, in a quick little gasp. 'I phoned at lunch time, but there was no one there.'

'I was down at the hospital getting plastered,' Charlie said. Then he took in what her words meant. 'You phoned at *lunch time*? Why weren't you in school?'

'I sneaked out,' Rachel said breathlessly. 'I wanted to ask you—'

She stopped. Charlie waited a moment, but nothing else came down the phone. 'What did you want?' he said at last, quite kindly.

Rachel gave an awkward little laugh. 'Well . . . it was about Peter. Peter Luttrell.'

Charlie stopped smiling. 'Tell me.'

'He just . . . freaked out,' said Rachel. Her voice trembled.

'Go on.'

'He was eating his sandwiches in the library. And you know how strict Mrs Ramm is about that. So Zoë went over to tell him.'

Charlie closed his eyes. 'You mean she went to hassle him.'

'She *is* a librarian,' Rachel said, defensively. 'It was her job. She just told him that he'd get into really serious trouble. And that it's silly to take food in when the books cost so much and it's so easy to damage them, and—'

'OK, OK.' Charlie could just imagine it. Zoë the guardian of common sense. Avenging and self-righteous. Barging over to Peter and thrusting her podgy face up to his, too close. 'So what happened? Did he go for Zoë?'

'No. It wasn't like that at all.' Rachel laughed again, nervously. 'It sounds silly, but it was as if—' She swallowed, and there was a long silence. Then she said, 'I thought he'd died.'

'You mean he fainted?'

'Of course not,' Rachel said. 'Fainting's not scary. We did that on our First Aid course. And he didn't fall over or anything. He just sat in the back corner with his eyes rolled up, all stiff. And his hands—'

Her voice cracked, and Charlie remembered that she was only eleven. She sounded very frightened. 'What did you do?' he said, as gently as he could.

'Well, Zoë got Mrs Ramm, of course. And she—well, she was worried, I think. When we couldn't wake Peter up, she called an ambulance and they took him off to St Martha's. And sent for his parents.'

Charlie looked down at his fingers, clasped round the telephone. He had a sudden sharp image of them holding a camera. Pointing it at a pair of strange, dark eyes. Thoughts roared in his brain. 'What happened then?'

'I don't know,' Rachel said. She was crying now. 'We don't even know if he's still alive. And Zoë won't do anything. But I thought . . . you're friendly with Jennifer, aren't you?'

So that was it. 'You want me to find out how Peter is?'

'Yes, please.' Rachel sniffed.

'All right. Stay there, and I'll call you back in a minute.'

Charlie put the receiver down and picked up the phone book. As he turned the pages, images shuffled in his mind. Peter. The otter. The otter out in the river, free and alive and fast. Peter in the library. *I thought he'd died . . .*

He dialled the number, and Jennifer answered, sharp and brisk.

'Yes?'

'It's me. Charlie. I've just heard about what happened to Peter. How is he?'

'He's fine,' Jennifer said shortly.

'What did they think it was?'

'It was nothing. OK?' Jennifer was almost snapping now. 'He just fainted or something, and Mum and Dad brought him straight home when they got to the hospital. Bye.'

She put the phone down before he could speak again.

Charlie stared at it for a moment, and then he phoned Rachel back. She was so grateful and relieved that it was a good ten minutes before he could go back to the darkroom.

Chapter Eighteen

When he went into school on Tuesday, Charlie found out what had really happened. There were people whispering everywhere.

Zoë Carter went crazy. He was eating his lunch in the library, and there was pâté smeared all over that new bird book. And tangerine juice on the big Shakespeare. And...

At first break, he went looking for Zoë.

It was one of her days for library duty, and she was up by the Literature shelves, looking aggressively efficient as she bustled round tidying. Charlie sat down at a table and watched her.

'What are you staring at?' she said.

'I'm wondering why you're so keen to get Peter Luttrell into trouble.'

'Me? I don't know what you're talking about.' Zoë turned her back and straightened a book that didn't need straightening.

'Oh yes, you do. He would never have messed up books like that. Someone must have ... helped him.'

'Don't be silly!' Zoë snapped. She was defiant and angry. 'Peter's off his head. He vandalized all those books and then he went loopy because he was scared when I caught him.'

'What reason would he have for doing something like that?'

'I can't read his mind,' said Zoë loftily.

Charlie let her tidy another shelf. Then he said, very softly, '*You* smeared pâté and things on those books, didn't you?'

She was very still for a second. Then she whirled round and glared at him. 'What rubbish! Why should I go round ruining books? I'm a librarian. The trouble with you is that you think Peter Luttrell can't do anything wrong. He's bewitched you!'

She was working herself up into a frenzy of righteous indignation, breathing fast and turning red in the face. Charlie could see that he wasn't going to get any sense out of her. He stood up and walked away.

As he passed the office, he saw that Mrs Ramm was inside, leafing slowly through the new bird book. He pushed the door open.

'Yes?' Mrs Ramm said.

Charlie pointed at the book. 'Is it bad?'

She held it out for him to see. The pages had been wiped clean of pâté, but they were damp and crinkled, and one of the colour plates was stained. 'It's not in prime condition,' she said.

'Will . . . the person who did it have to pay for it?' Charlie muttered.

Mrs Ramm gave him a shrewd look. 'If I can prove who did do it.'

'And you can't?'

She shrugged. 'There are only three people who know exactly what happened, and two of them are telling the same story.'

Charlie had been afraid of that. 'Zoë and Rachel?'

Mrs Ramm nodded. 'I'm not a fool. I've heard Zoë goading that poor child before. But I can't prove anything, and they're backing each other up. If I say what I think, it'll just mean a row with their parents.'

'Their mum would be furious. She's always on their side.' Charlie could imagine Alison's reaction if she thought her children were being unjustly accused. She and Zoë were very like each other.

Mrs Ramm's mouth tightened. 'Peter's parents came to the hospital. They didn't strike me as being . . . over-indulgent.'

'No,' Charlie said. 'They're not.'

Mrs Ramm sighed. 'Maybe I'll forget about making anyone pay for the damage. This time.'

Standing up, she led the way out of the office. As Charlie left the library, he could hear her giving instructions to Zoë, as crisp and impersonal as ever. He wished he could be like that, and behave as though nothing had happened.

But he couldn't. At lunch time, he cornered Rachel coming out of the dining room. It was a good opportunity, because Zoë was still at the counter, choosing her meal. She would be busy for twenty minutes at least.

'I want to talk to you.'

Rachel looked wary, but Charlie didn't wait for questions. He hustled her round behind the French mobile, where the new pond was being dug. She pulled a face as she picked her way across the sticky brown clay.

'Why've we got to talk here? It's disgusting.'

'That's why,' Charlie said grimly. 'I don't want to be disturbed.'

Rachel looked up nervously.

Charlie nodded. 'You didn't tell me that Zoë got into one of her rages. That business yesterday was all her fault, wasn't it?'

'I . . . ' Rachel gulped and stopped.

'I know what she's like,' Charlie said. 'Remember that time she thought you'd hidden her hairbrush?'

She had flown into a frenzy. Convinced that she was right, and determined to make Rachel admit it. Whatever she had to do.

Rachel gave an odd moan.

'Tell me what really happened yesterday,' Charlie murmured.

'I . . . he . . . it was Peter's fault,' said Rachel wretchedly. 'Zoë didn't mean to get him into trouble. She only told him to put his lunch away, so he didn't mess the books up. If he'd done what she said—'

'What did he do?'

'He just stared.' Rachel's voice trembled uncertainly. 'And when Zoë said he would get into trouble with Mrs Ramm, he . . . '

'Yes?' Charlie said. Insisting.

'He sort of . . . smiled. As if he knew better.'

She stopped and looked down and Charlie drew a long, deep breath. 'But *no one* knows better than Zoë. Isn't that right? So she had to prove that he would get into trouble.'

Rachel nodded, hanging her head. 'And once she'd started—'

'She couldn't stop.' Charlie could imagine it. 'I bet you were frightened.'

Rachel nodded again. 'What are you going to do?' she whispered. 'Zoë'll kill me if I tell Mrs Ramm.'

'That's not the answer anyway.' Charlie was working it out. 'If there's a big row, it'll just cause more trouble for Peter. Zoë has to make it up some other way. Like—' Suddenly, he saw the perfect solution. He grinned at Rachel. 'I'm going to make her apologize to Peter. Is he here today?'

Rachel shook her head. She looked awed at the idea. Charlie grinned again.

'We'll go round after school then. It'll teach her a lesson.'

* * *

He never had any doubt that he could make Zoë do it.

'If you don't, I'll *force* Rachel to tell Mrs Ramm the truth. Then you'll have to pay for the books. And you'll lose your librarian's badge.'

'Don't care,' Zoë said, sulkily.

But she did care, and Charlie knew it. She liked being Sensible Zoë Carter, the girl the teachers relied on. Losing her librarian's badge would spoil all that. So she didn't protest when Charlie came up beside her as she was walking out of school. And she didn't go on up the hill, heading home. She turned towards River Walk, without making a scene.

'I'm not grovelling, mind,' she muttered defiantly.

'You don't need to grovel.' Charlie couldn't think of anything more repulsive. 'Just say you're sorry you lost your temper. And tell him he won't have to pay for the books.'

Zoë looked up quickly. 'But Mrs Ramm—'

'Mrs Ramm's no fool,' Charlie said. 'She may not be able to prove what happened, but you don't think you took her in, do you?'

That shut Zoë up. She walked the rest of the way in silence, until they came round the bend in River Walk and saw the Luttrells' house. Then she gave a little squeak.

'It's weird!'

It was more than weird. Mr Luttrell hadn't stopped at boarding up the front gate. The whole place looked like a prison. The boarded gate at the front was clamped shut with a padlock, and topped with barbed wire. And there was more barbed wire running in curls along the garden wall, held in place by heavy staples. Charlie felt as though a cold hand had clutched the back of his neck.

But he wasn't going to side with Zoë. 'Come on,' he hissed. He led the way into the front garden and when the door opened, he was ready with his best smile. 'Hallo, Mrs Luttrell. We've come to see Peter.'

Mrs Luttrell blinked at them. She was paler than he remembered, with dark smudges under her eyes. 'I'm not sure if he can—'

'We've got messages,' Charlie said firmly. 'Haven't we, Zoë? It won't take a minute.'

There was an awkward pause, and then Mrs Luttrell stepped back. 'He's up in his bedroom. Doing homework or something. The doctor said he ought to stay off school today. Just in case . . . ' Her voice trailed away vaguely and she waved them in. 'It's the front room. At the end of the landing.'

Charlie climbed the stairs, with Zoë trailing behind him. He expected Peter's door to be tightly shut, like the shed door, but it was wide open. As he reached the top of the staircase, he turned, to walk along the landing, and saw Peter at the far end, sitting at a table under the window. He was studying a big sheet of paper, leaning his elbows on it to stop it rolling up.

'Hi,' Charlie said.

At the sound of his voice, Peter looked round, eagerly. 'I've done it!' he called. 'I've spent the whole day working on it—and it's finished!'

Chapter Nineteen

For a second, Charlie didn't understand. Then he realized what Peter meant, and he ran down the landing, leaving Zoë behind.

'You've done the map?'

Peter nodded. Leaning back, he lifted his elbows, so that the paper curled up, into a long white roll. He didn't say anything else until Charlie was in the room. Then he spoke again, almost in a whisper.

'I've done everything I could think of. I don't think I've missed anything out, but it's been . . . impossible to get out and check. I had to do most of it from memory.'

Charlie took a long, deep breath. 'Can I look?'

'If you like.'

Walking across the room, Charlie picked up the stiff paper. Peter watched him, with an unreadable expression. His nervous fingers moved restlessly, fiddling with a piece of Blu-tack that he took off the table.

The river ran right across the paper in a great blue loop. The rest of the map was completely covered with fine, pencilled writing in little balloons. There must have been several hundred of them, each one with an arrow pointing to the appropriate part of the river. There wasn't time to read more than one or two.

> old badger sett. safe in day.
> dogs here. bad place to land.
> chub under bank. out of current. angry swans.
> good slipway. deep water.

The points of the arrows clustered on both banks of the river and sometimes in the middle too, running from one side of the paper to the other. They tailed off towards the west, by the sewage works—

sewage outflow. foul water and no fish

—but everywhere else they crowded along the blue strip. Hundreds of intricate, secret details. If the whole river had been blown up that night, it could have been reconstructed from the map, all the way from the alder pool to the sewage works.

'Is it what you wanted?' Peter said. His eyes were on Charlie's face, and his hands were pulling and pinching at the Blu-tack.

'It's wonderful,' Charlie said, still staring down. 'It's going to take me weeks to read it all, but—yes, it's brilliant. Thanks very much.'

'So you'll take some more pictures?' Peter said eagerly. Almost greedily.

'Lots.' Charlie looked up and grinned. 'Do you still want some?'

Peter nodded. 'I . . . like your pictures,' he said slowly. 'They . . . remind me of how the river really is. If I can't—'

And then he looked over Charlie's shoulder and saw Zoë. She had come down the landing, and she was standing in the doorway. The moment Peter caught sight of her, his eagerness vanished. For an instant he froze, with a jerk that snapped the Blu-tack he was holding. Then he swivelled away and bent over the table.

'It's all right,' Charlie said. 'She's come to apologize.'

Peter hunched forward, without answering. Catching hold of Zoë's elbow, Charlie pulled her into the room and closed the door. Then he kicked her ankle.

'Go on!' he hissed. 'Say it!'

She must have been rehearsing the words in her head. They came out without hesitation, in a stiff, chilly monotone that made Charlie wince.

'I'm very sorry about what happened in the library. It won't happen again. And Mrs Ramm won't make you pay for the books.'

Peter gave no sign that he had heard. Picking up a pencil, he began to scribble on a piece of paper. The pencil point scratched drily.

'Peter?' Charlie put out a hand and touched the bony shoulder in front of him. Peter flinched sideways, and Charlie had a brief glimpse of the random loops that he had scrawled. Then Peter snatched the paper away and there was nothing at all on the table.

Except—

'What's that?' Zoë said. In quite a different voice.

It was the piece of Blu-tack. Peter had moulded it into the shape of a tiny man, but when he froze, at the sight of Zoë, he had pulled off one of the feet. The left leg was incomplete, hanging in a tiny blue stump.

Charlie had only a second to see what it was like before Peter's hand shot out and snatched that up too. He squashed the Blu-tack into a shapeless lump and twisted away from Charlie and Zoë, huddling over with his back to them.

Zoë opened her mouth.

'Don't you dare!' Charlie muttered.

He could see that she was going to make a scene, and he didn't dare to imagine what would happen if she did it here, in the Luttrells' house. He grabbed her hand and pulled her away from the table.

'But didn't you see—?' she hissed.

'Be quiet!' Charlie seized the librarian's badge on the front of her sweatshirt and dragged it up to her face. 'Just concentrate on keeping this, and don't worry about anything else.' He looked over his shoulder at Peter. 'She won't bother you any more.'

Peter sat very still, with his back to them, his fingers tapping the table.

'We're off then,' Charlie said, tucking the map under his arm. 'Come on, Zoë. And make sure you say goodbye to Peter's mother. Politely.'

Zoë swept downstairs, with a smile that put Charlie's into the shade. 'Thank you so much for letting us in, Mrs Luttrell. We got everything sorted out.'

But the moment they were away from the house, she rounded on Charlie.

'You see?' she said fiercely. 'I was right all along, wasn't I? He's *evil*!'

A cold weight settled in Charlie's throat. Zoë thrust her face up close to his.

'Didn't you see what was on his desk? It's proof. Absolute proof!'

'I don't know what you're talking about,' Charlie said. But he did. Suddenly he saw the desk with Zoë's eyes, and he knew what she had picked on.

She nodded triumphantly. 'That figure. That's what witches make, to stick pins in. An effigy.'

'Oh, for heaven's sake! It was only a bit of Blu-tack. Just something he was fiddling with.'

'You can't see it, can you?' Zoë was hard and scornful. 'He's really got you in his power.'

'Oh, for heaven's sake!' Charlie's patience suddenly snapped. He didn't care that they were in the street, where anyone could see them. He didn't care that Zoë was his cousin, and younger than he was. He just knew that she was being pigheaded and unkind. Seizing her shoulders, he shook her, hard, jerking her head backwards and forwards.

'Leave Peter alone!' he panted. 'He's got enough to bear, without you sticking your fat nose into things. LEAVE HIM ALONE.'

When he let her go, she was gasping and crying, but she hadn't given in. She lifted her head and gave him a long, steady stare.

'You see?' she said.

Then she walked off up the hill, leaving Charlie feeling powerless and wretched.

Chapter Twenty

He knew something terrible was going to happen. For a week, he felt it gathering in the school. People whispering in corners. Looking through doors at him as they passed in the corridor. Suddenly falling silent when he walked into a room. But it wasn't anything he could catch hold of and investigate.

He tried quizzing Keith one day, when they were walking home, pretending to make a joke of it.

'What's the great plot then? It feels as if the whole school's been taken over by the CIA.'

'Plot?' Keith's eyes shifted uneasily.

'Oh, come on.' Charlie laughed, but he could hear the false, self-conscious ring of it. 'You could cut the air with a knife. It's clotted with conspiracy.'

'Just the usual gossip,' Keith said lightly. Still not looking at him. 'Plans to spy on the teachers and blow up the staffroom.' His laugh was as false as Charlie's. 'Where d'you think we ought to plant the bombs?'

It was an invitation to duck out into one of their elaborate fantasy schemes, but Charlie couldn't do it. He stopped dead and stared until Keith was forced to look him in the eye.

Then he said, 'You've got to tell me. I have to know.'

'Know what?' Keith said. 'The riddle of the universe?'

It was Charlie's last chance to cop out. To preserve their safe, jokey friendship. He made himself not take it. Forced himself to speak directly.

'Look, I know everyone's talking about Peter and this rubbish of Zoë's. I'm not an idiot. But they don't really believe it, do they?'

'Well . . . ' Keith shrugged awkwardly. 'They don't and they do. You know how it is.'

He was starting to edge away. Charlie could feel him hating the whole conversation, but he couldn't let him go yet. He caught hold of his sleeve.

'So what are they going to do?' he said urgently. 'What's going to *happen*?'

'Nothing's going to happen,' Keith said irritably. He pulled his arm free and brushed at his sleeve.

'There's no plan?'

'Of course there isn't a plan. You really are paranoid, aren't you? What's got into you?'

He didn't wait for an answer. Spinning round, he strode away, so fast that Charlie would have had to jog to catch him up.

But there wouldn't have been any point in catching him up. Charlie stood and watched him disappear round the corner. Then, very slowly, he walked after him.

He never doubted, for a moment, that Keith had told him the truth. There was no definite plan to injure Peter. But that just made things worse. If there'd been a plan, there would have been the possibility of foiling it. As it was, he couldn't do anything except wait for the explosion.

It took another week. And when it happened, it was completely random and casual. Peter was walking out of school on Friday with everyone else, separate—because he was always separate—but surrounded by people. Charlie was a hundred metres or so behind, but he saw what happened. Everybody saw what happened.

The girl in front of Peter stopped without warning, to tie her shoelace, and he stumbled into her and stepped on her bag. There was a crunch, and a black stain began to seep across the surface of the bag.

'You've broken my ink!' the girl yelled. She jumped up and thumped him. 'You clumsy little—'

And then she saw who it was that she had thumped.

Anyone else would have been apologizing or arguing or thumping her back. But Peter had frozen, with his eyes fixed on her face. Staring.

And she froze too. For a moment, there was a pool of silence round the two of them. Charlie began to walk faster, not knowing what was going to happen, but feeling the tension rise all round him. He was trying to reach Peter before anything happened.

But he didn't make it. Suddenly, Zoë darted forward and prodded Peter hard in the ribs with one outstretched finger.

'Leave her alone!' she shouted. 'Stop *eyeing* her.'

If Peter had stayed frozen, it might still have been all right. But he wavered, just for an instant, flinching away from her finger. And that was enough to start the whole thing off. Suddenly, everyone was diving at him. Prodding him. Tweaking his tie. Pulling at his clothes.

'Stop eyeing!'

'Stop giving her the evil eye!'

'Evil Eye!'

All the suspicion and uneasiness that had been brewing for weeks boiled over in a surge of hostility. His bag flew out of the middle of the crowd and was flung from hand to hand, spilling papers everywhere. His jacket was torn off and his shirt ripped open between two sets of wrenching hands. And then he went over on to the tarmac and dozens of screaming people piled in on top of him.

Evil Eye! Evil Eye! Evil Eye!

Charlie was there at the edge of the crowd, trying to fight his way in, but there were bigger, heavier people in front of him. An elbow crashed into his face, and someone knocked him over and stepped on his fingers. All he could see of Peter was one trouser-leg, ripped and dusty, and a raw, red knee. He could feel his own voice shouting, 'Stop it! Stop it!' but the sound was lost in the roar all round him.

Evil Eye! Evil Eye!

It felt unstoppable—except by something so appalling that people would be shocked into silence. Grovelling under the battering fists, Charlie was truly afraid, for the first time in his life.

And then it was all ended, by a single word. Yelled loud enough for everyone to hear.

'Frankenstein!'

Suddenly, there were scrambling feet all round Charlie, as people ran off through the gate. Hauling himself up, he saw that Jennifer had done what he ought to have had the sense to do himself. She was running round the bend in the drive with Mr Feinstein close behind her.

Peter was curled up tight, with his hands up to protect his head. Charlie bent down and touched him on the shoulder.

'It's OK. Everyone's gone.'

Warily, Peter lifted his head and looked round. Then he began to get up. When Mr Feinstein arrived, he was on his feet, looking dirty and sullen.

'So what's been going on here?' Mr Feinstein looked him up and down. 'Must have been quite a fight.'

'It wasn't a fight,' Charlie said hotly. 'It was a massacre. Peter was—'

Mr Feinstein waved him away. 'If it was his massacre, let him tell me about it. Well, Luttrell?'

Peter stared up at him, blankly.

'Well?' This time, there was a touch of impatience in Mr Feinstein's voice. 'What did you do?'

'I broke someone's ink,' Peter said. 'In her bag.'

His voice was flat and unemotional. Charlie leapt in to try and make Mr Feinstein understand.

'It wasn't his fault! It was an accident. And then everyone piled in. It was dreadful—'

Mr Feinstein's voice interrupted him. Cold and unimpressed. 'And why did they do that?'

'Because—'

And then Charlie saw the trap he'd fallen into. It was impossible to explain about the Evil Eye. Mr Feinstein would never understand that. Charlie broke off and dropped his head.

Mr Feinstein sighed irritably. 'I don't seem to be getting any answers. Jennifer came racing into the staffroom shrieking about emergencies, but there's no emergency here. If you're not going to tell me what happened, there's nothing I can do.'

'You don't need to do anything,' Jennifer muttered. 'The fight's over, and Peter's fine. Aren't you, Peter?'

Peter nodded and straightened his tie, tucking his torn shirt back into his trousers. Jennifer picked up his bag and started collecting the scattered papers that were blowing up and down the drive.

Mr Feinstein gave them a sharp look. 'I ought to give your parents a ring. They'll want to know why Peter's come home in that state.'

Jennifer whirled round, thrusting the last bundle of papers into the bag. 'It's all right,' she said quickly. 'They'll be round at our grandmother's. I can sort all this out before they get home.' She caught hold of Peter's elbow and began to hustle him away down the drive.

Mr Feinstein watched them go. 'I don't think there's much harm done,' he said, half to himself.

'You're not going to leave it like that?' Charlie couldn't believe his ears.

Mr Feinstein sighed. 'You're a nice boy, Willcox. Honest. Well-meaning. But you're naïve. If those two don't want me to phone their parents, it's because they know the fight was Peter's fault.'

'No it's not!' Charlie said. 'You don't understand—'

'Sometimes it's better not to interfere. Why don't you leave them to sort themselves out?' Mr Feinstein's voice wasn't unkind, but it was final. He turned and strode back up the drive, leaving Charlie standing on his own.

Wearily, Charlie picked up his own bag from the grass where he'd dropped it when he plunged into the fight. He was just going to walk off when he saw a last, lone sheet of paper blowing away from him. A bit that Jennifer had missed.

He jogged after it and picked it up, in case it was important. But he wasn't keen to go round to the Luttrells' house unless he had to, so he glanced down at the writing, to see what it was.

And it knocked the breath out of him.

Chapter Twenty-One

It was a poem. The title—*My Bedroom*—was written neatly across the top of the front page.

A Mrs Williams special, that. Dead imaginative. It was always the first homework she gave her classes, because she reckoned it was a way of getting to know them. Charlie remembered writing all about his cameras and the photographs on his wall.

There weren't any photographs in Peter's poem. No personal details of hobbies or interests. Mrs Williams had obviously been disappointed.

> *My bedroom—*
> *Soft duvet on the bed*
> *Clean white paint on the window sill*
> *Shelves of books*
> *Ornaments and soft cushions.*
>
> *Where I sleep—*
> *Darkness, deep darkness*
> *Hard and cold*
> *Lumpy mattress makes me*
> *Toss and turn.*
>
> *In there—*
> *It's warm and smells of roses*
> *With a night light like a little house*
> *And soft, soft pillows.*

Where I sleep—
The floor is hard
Spiders crawl in the corners
And the draught comes through the loose board
The only way out.

Charlie closed his eyes. He wished he hadn't read it. He wished he had let the piece of paper blow away across the field.

But he hadn't. He opened his eyes again and read what Mrs Williams had written at the bottom of the page. Her comments were crisp and practical.

An interesting way to deal with a nightmare, but I'd have liked a bit more detail. And you have used the word 'soft' four times. Please try to vary your vocabulary.

Oh, well done. Ten out of ten for that teacher. Charlie opened his bag and slipped the paper in.

When he got home, he stuck it on his bedroom wall, next to Peter's map. Then he lay down on the bed, gazing up at them both. He'd spent hours studying the map already. Trying to absorb all the details, so that the river ran live and glittering in his mind, just as it must in Peter's. Now he read the poem, over and over again, until he knew it by heart.

He wanted to *understand*.

On Saturday morning, he went looking for Jennifer.

He telephoned first, and Mrs Luttrell answered the phone, as anxious and apologetic as usual.

'I . . . oh dear, she's out, Charlie. I think she said she was going into town. She'll be in this afternoon, if you want to come round—'

'No, that's all right, Mrs Luttrell. I'll see if I can find her.'

He couldn't bear the idea of waiting. He walked into the middle of town and began working his way round the shops. Jennifer wasn't where he thought she might be, in Wilson's. Most of the Camera Club girls hung out there, reading catalogues and chatting up Stephen Wilson, but Jennifer wasn't one of them. She wasn't in any of the bookshops, either. Nor in the clothes shops round the library.

He caught sight of her at last, almost by accident, in the big garden centre next to Sainsbury's. She was just paying for a flat parcel in a paper bag. Charlie strolled in and whispered over her shoulder.

'What are you doing? Starting an allotment?'

She jerked round. When she saw who it was, she looked wary. 'You made me jump.'

'Sorry. I was coming to see if you fancied a coffee.'

There was a flicker of surprise, but she didn't argue. Maybe she guessed that he wasn't going to let her refuse. 'If you like.'

'Let's go to Kenworthy's,' Charlie said. 'We might get a bit of peace there, and it's got a better view than McDonald's.'

Ten minutes later, they were in the café up at the top of Kenworthy's, sitting at a window table. Jennifer sipped her cappuccino, frowning at Charlie over the cup.

Charlie pulled Peter's poem out of his bag and pushed it across the table. 'Read that.'

If Jennifer recognized the writing, she didn't show it. Her eyes skimmed the page and when she looked up, her face was carefully blank.

'So?'

Charlie reached over and tapped Peter's name, written at the top of the paper. 'It's . . . odd, isn't it?'

'Odd?' Jennifer's voice was elaborately casual. 'What's odd about it? Everyone has nightmares.'

She picked up a packet of sugar from the little dish in the centre of the table and began to fiddle with it, twisting it first one way and then the other.

'Is it just a nightmare?' Charlie said.

'I don't know what you're talking about,' Jennifer said. Stiff, but not puzzled. Charlie could tell that she knew exactly what he was talking about.

He took a deep breath. 'You got very strange once,' he said, 'when I made a joke about sleeping in the shed.'

Jennifer's hands went very still, poised over the table, with the sugar packet twisted tight between them. Charlie could see her trying to speak, but no words came.

'It's not you that sleeps in the shed, is it?' he said at last. 'It's Peter. He gets locked in, doesn't he? That's why the key's in the padlock.'

The moment the words were out, he couldn't believe he'd said them. He waited for Jennifer to look at him, goggle-eyed, and tell him he was crazy. But she didn't. Her eyes flicked quickly left and right, checking that no one had heard.

Then she said, 'You mustn't—' Her voice was quick and nervous. 'It's not like you think. He doesn't get beaten or . . . or anything.'

'But your dad locks him up out there?'

'It's not—you don't understand!'

'Of course I don't understand!' Charlie said angrily.

The woman at the next table looked round and he waited for her to turn away before he began again, more quietly.

'How can I understand something like that? Locking an eleven-year-old boy in a shed. All night.'

'He has to. He can't—' Suddenly, Jennifer began to talk fast. But so softly that Charlie had to lean half-way across the table to make out what she was saying. 'Dad can't share things. He keeps it all shut inside. He's had the most horrible time with Gran, because he never knows where she's going to get to next, or what she's going to do. But he's never moaned. Not once.'

'So what am I supposed to do? Admire him?'

It was Jennifer's turn to look angry. 'You haven't got a clue, have you? Can't you imagine what it's like for him? Gran's getting worse and worse. He can't keep the animal out of the garden. And Peter drives him crazy. He's like a piece of elastic, stretched as tight as it will go. If he didn't put Peter in the shed, he *would* hit him.'

'Maybe Peter would rather be hit,' Charlie said fiercely. 'This isn't doing him much good, is it? Why d'you *think* he's so weird?'

'That's rubbish! He was always weird!'

Charlie didn't say anything. He just waited. Jennifer struggled for a minute and then she dropped her head and went on.

'No, that's not fair. He's never got on with Dad. They've always rubbed each other up the wrong way. But since Gran got ill . . . ' She rubbed a hand across her face. 'The first time he put Peter outside, it was a relief. Because I was so scared of what he might do otherwise.'

'Didn't you *say* anything?' Charlie couldn't imagine standing by while something like that was going on.

'I didn't know it would keep happening, did I? And it didn't happen very often at first, only when Peter was really annoying. But then the footprints started, and Dad just can't handle it all. He can't take the way the thing's still getting in, in spite of the barbed wire. He's beginning . . . ' Her mouth pinched tight for a moment, and then she made herself go on. 'He's beginning to talk about it as if it's magic or something.'

She was fiddling with the sugar again, winding it tighter and tighter in her fingers. Charlie stared at the packet too. He didn't know what to say.

'I've heard him wake up in the night,' Jennifer muttered. 'He whispers to Mum. On and on, about how the thing's spreading germs. And when it dug up the flowerbeds—'

The paper split suddenly. Sugar poured out on to the table cloth and Jennifer broke off, staring down at it.

'Do you think he needs a doctor?' Charlie said gently.

'He needs to get rid of that *animal*!' Fiercely, Jennifer began to spoon the sugar into her coffee. 'And we've nearly done it.'

She bent down suddenly and picked up the paper bag from the garden centre, pushing it across the table to Charlie.

'He sent me out to buy this. We're going to make a trap. And when we've caught it, everything will be all right! Please don't start interfering now.'

Charlie opened the bag and looked in. It was full of black netting. Very strong and thick.

'I'm going to make it into a bag,' Jennifer said. 'Dad's thinking where he can put it so that the mink gets tangled up in it. Then we can take it to a zoo, or dump it a long way away.'

Charlie pulled a bit of netting out of the bag. Winding it round his hands he tugged, hard. The black threads bit into his flesh.

'It won't break,' Jennifer said. 'It's nylon.' She took the netting away from Charlie and pushed it back into the bag. 'Don't tell anyone about Peter and the shed. Let's see if this works first.'

'But I can't just ignore—'

'Please! Just a few weeks. Until the end of term!'

Charlie felt as if he were balanced on a high wire, over deep water. Whichever way he slipped, he would be in out of his depth.

'Well . . . ' he said slowly.

Jennifer smiled and reached out for his hand. But before she touched it, a voice boomed across the café.

'What are you two doing lounging round here?'

It was Mr Feinstein. He was swooping towards them with a cup of coffee in one hand and a vast sticky bun in the other.

'You shouldn't be wasting time drinking coffee,' he called. 'You ought to be out working on your photo essays. There's not much time left.'

Jennifer whipped up her jacket. 'I've got to go,' she hissed. 'Remember . . . you promised.'

'But—'

Charlie glanced sideways, at Mr Feinstein. When he looked back, Jennifer was half-way to the exit. He saw her lips move, mouthing something at him.

Until the end of term . . .

Chapter Twenty-Two

'What's wrong with Jennifer?' Mr Feinstein said, lowering himself into the chair she had just left. 'Can't she cope with teachers in real life?'

'This is real life?' Charlie was relieved that his voice didn't shake. '*Kenworthy's?*'

Mr Feinstein pulled a face at him. 'Don't knock it. They've got the best Danish pastries in town. And the best view of the river.'

The second thing was certainly true. They were sitting on the fourth floor, with the Old Bridge almost directly beneath them, and they could see a great arc of the river, stretching away up to the castle.

'Yes, it is good,' Charlie said.

Mr Feinstein grinned. 'Only place you can see two miles of the river, all at once. And it's even better from the roof garden. Up there, you can see right round to the sewage works. And all along the back of River Walk, as well.'

Charlie was still looking out of the window, trying to catch sight of Jennifer as she came out of Kenworthy's front door. 'Roof garden?' he said vaguely.

'Up there.' Mr Feinstein stopped tipping sugar into his coffee and used his spoon to point at the ceiling.

'A *garden*?' Charlie said. 'On the roof?'

'The full works. Didn't you know? Rose bushes and honeysuckle and little box hedges. They used to serve teas up there in the summer, but there was a silly scare about safety and they closed it. "Temporarily". Must be fifteen years ago now.' He picked up his bun and took a huge bite. 'You ought to try and get up there.'

'Me?' Charlie was watching Jennifer walk out on to the bridge, with the paper bag tucked under her arm. 'What for?'

'Oh, come on!' Mr Feinstein sounded impatient. 'I've seen some of those pictures you've got for your photo essay. Fiddly little details. They're fine, but they'd be much stronger if you had something to pull them together. An overview of the river.'

'Maybe—'

Maybe a map? Charlie was going to say. But he stopped. He didn't want to talk to Mr Feinstein about Peter's map.

Mr Feinstein didn't even notice that he'd spoken. He swept on, in full flood. 'You'd get a wonderful overview from the roof garden. I thought of it as soon as I saw you sitting here.'

So that was why he'd come crashing across the café.

'I thought it was supposed to be a personal essay,' Charlie said. He wasn't sure he wanted to be taken over like that. 'You told us to look at things in our own way.'

'Of course I did.' Mr Feinstein lifted his coffee cup. 'I'm not telling you what to see. I'm just suggesting somewhere that might interest you. I can get you permission to go up there, if you like.' He grinned. 'Unless you'd rather sit in here and do your homework.'

He reached across for the piece of paper that Jennifer had left lying on the table. Charlie snatched at it, but too late. Mr Feinstein was holding it in both hands, studying the name at the top.

'Interesting,' he said lightly. 'A good image for nightmares.'

'Not surprising he has nightmares,' Charlie said. 'Considering how people treat him.' He meant to stop there, but he was annoyed. His voice went on, before he could stop himself. 'You were wrong about that fight. It wasn't his fault at all.'

Mr Feinstein gave him a long stare. 'Maybe I should have asked a few more questions,' he said.

'Of course you should,' Charlie said bitterly. 'But you didn't bother—because you don't like Peter. He gets under your skin, doesn't he? You don't know about his family—'

Mr Feinstein lifted a hand. 'I can't discuss Peter with you. It wouldn't be professional.'

'Professional!' Charlie said scornfully. He snatched the poem back. 'That's why it's no use talking to teachers in real life. You don't *care*.'

'Come on, now. You don't understand—'

'Everyone keeps telling me I don't understand. Well, I'm going to make sure I do. I'm going to check the facts, the way you should have done.'

Charlie stood up and marched out of the café, with the folder under his arm. He knew, now, what he had to do.

It was the sort of plan he'd made a hundred times when he was younger, imagining himself sneaking out in the dark. It used to be so vivid that he could almost hear the stairs creak and feel the carpet under his bare feet.

The only difference was that, this time, it was real. He didn't fall asleep before he could start. He undressed and went to bed, but his brain was churning, and each tiny noise rang in his ears. He heard his parents settling down in bed. Heard the hum of the washing machine turning itself on with the automatic switch, at half past one. Heard the night plane from the airport that went over at around two.

At three o'clock, he was as wide awake as he had been all day, and he knew that he was really going to do it. He slid out of bed, pulled on jeans and a jumper, and picked up his trainers.

It was just as easy as he'd always imagined. He crept downstairs, avoiding the two steps that creaked, lifted his coat off the hook and picked up a torch. A minute later, he was outside the back door with the key in his pocket.

Everything was very still, except for the occasional car rushing past. He walked briskly, with his head down, working out details. The wrought-iron gate at the front of the Luttrells' garden was padlocked. There would be no way in there. But it was much harder to padlock the back gate. Maybe he could get in through that.

As he went over the Old Bridge, he heard the lonely, liquid sound of the river against the stonework. For a moment, he wondered idly whether there was any way of photographing that noise. Of inventing a picture that conjured up the slow, flat *slap, slap, slap*. But his mind wouldn't play games. The only picture it made was the dark wooden shed. With the key hanging from its padlock.

The moon was very bright along River Walk. It caught the coils of barbed wire along the wall, throwing strange, elongated shadows over the bricks as Charlie slid down the alley. He didn't need the torch until he got to the river bank at the back.

Even then, he kept it pointed well down, towards the ground, as he reached over the barbed wire on top of the gate, feeling for a padlock. There didn't seem to be one, but when he pressed the latch, it wouldn't move. For a moment, he thought he'd come for nothing.

Then he shone the torch over the top and saw the thick wire wound round and round the latch. So that was what Mr

Luttrell had done. It was a fine defence against an animal, but it wouldn't stop him. Ignoring the barbs that scratched his wrists, Charlie untwisted the tangle and went through the gate, shutting it carefully behind him.

Inside the garden, everything was very dark. He turned the torch off and walked across to the shed, feeling for the padlock. The key was there, and it turned smoothly, well-oiled. Charlie slid the padlock apart and opened the door.

Inside, the smell of creosote mingled with something dry and musty, like the scent of a hamster's cage. Not unpleasant, but animal. Turning on the torch again, Charlie shone it round slowly, so that the light caught the spiders' webs up by the roof and the narrow board hanging slightly crooked in the back corner.

. . . the draught comes through the loose board
The only way out . . .

There was a pile of flower pots in one corner, lying against a heap of old sacks. Over on the other side was the mattress, with the blankets piled on top. For a moment, Charlie thought that was all there was and he felt himself relax. Not tonight.

And then the blankets stirred.

It was only the very faintest movement, but it set his heart thudding. 'Peter?'

There was no answer.

Slowly, forcing every step, Charlie made himself walk across to the mattress. The blankets were quite still now. He reached out his free hand and took hold of the thick cloth, lifting it cautiously.

Peter was underneath the blankets, curled up tight like someone asleep. But he wasn't asleep. His body was tense, and his eyes were wide open and remote, staring into nothing. They didn't blink when Charlie shone the torch at them. And when he stretched out his hand, feeling sick and terrified, to touch the cold cheek, there was no reaction at all. Not even the automatic twitch of a sleeping person.

Sliding his fingers down Peter's arm, over the small, flexed muscles, Charlie found the pulse at the wrist. It was ticking faintly but quite steadily.

So—not dead. But not sleeping, either. What then? Drugged?

Before he could answer his own question, there was a faint noise from behind. A rustle. Spinning round, he saw a dark shape rearing up out of the pile of old sacks.

For an instant it stared at him with wild, alien eyes, its shape clear in the torchlight. Round head. Straight, muscular body. Strong, tapering tail. Then, with a clack of wood on wood, it turned and pushed the loose board aside, slipping out into the darkness.

Charlie looked back at Peter, willing him to move. Willing him to smile and sit up. But there was no change in the blank, set face.

Then the otter whistled.

It was a long, high-pitched squeak, like nothing Charlie had ever heard before, but he knew what it was at once. And he remembered the closed gate, and the barbed wire. For an animal like that, there was no way out to the river.

Unless he helped it.

He made himself stand up and walk out of the shed. The garden looked empty, but his eyes found the otter crouched in the bushes beside the gate. Its head was lifted, staring up at the latch.

'Yes,' Charlie said. 'It's all right.'

He walked to the gate and bent down. The otter reared up, pushing against his hand with the top of its head. He felt the strong, waterproof hairs and, under them, the thin, rounded shape of the skull.

. . . their skulls are exceptionally fragile . . .

No need to wonder what it wanted. The longing flowed into his fingertips and up his arm. He straightened and unfastened the gate.

The moment there was a gap, the otter brushed past him with a soft 'hah!', its warm, solid weight knocking against his legs. He watched it slip out and lollop the short distance to the edge of the river.

It disappeared over the bank, hitting the water with such an immediate splash that it must have gone down in a single slide. Charlie imagined the slithery surface of the bare mud, and then the freshness of the water, and the long stream of silver bubbles escaping into the air.

Going back to the shed, he shone his torch in. Peter hadn't moved. He was still curled up under the blankets, his eyes wide and entranced. Charlie knew it would be no use shaking him, or shouting. He wouldn't stir. In some inexplicable way, he was—not there.

All the same, it was hard to lock him in again. Even though he knew it was the safe, sensible thing to do, Charlie had to force himself to close the door and click the padlock shut.

He walked out on to the river bank and reached over the gate, to find the wire he had untwisted. As his fingers closed round it, he turned and shone his torch on to the water.

He could see the otter, already a hundred yards upstream. It was swimming strongly, making for Toller's Mill and the alder pool.

. . . shallow crossing. badger track. old apple tree.

Charlie watched until he couldn't see it any longer. Then he pulled the gate almost shut, leaving the wire hanging, and turned off his torch. Slowly, he began to walk back, up the alley.

Chapter Twenty-Three

The first thing he did, when he woke up in the morning, was choose the best of his otter pictures. He put it into an envelope, with the poem from Peter's folder and another piece of paper that said *See you at the alder pool. 4.30 pm Wednesday. Charlie.* On Monday, he took the envelope to school.

When everyone else had gone to registration, he slipped into the Year Seven cloakroom and walked down the row of pegs, looking for Peter's coat. When he'd checked the name tape at the back of the neck, he slid his envelope into the pocket. A stiff square that Peter couldn't possibly miss. He was about to leave, when someone spoke to him from the corridor.

'Willcox? Is that you?'

Charlie spun round. Mr Feinstein was standing there, looking down the row of pegs at him.

'Yes, sir?'

'I was on my way to find you,' Mr Feinstein said. 'To give you this.'

He held out an envelope. For one surreal moment, Charlie thought it was his own, magically transferred from Peter's pocket. Then he saw that it was narrower, and already opened. He walked up the cloakroom and held out his hand.

'What is it?'

'It's what I promised you,' Mr Feinstein said. He grinned. 'Just to show there's no hard feelings.'

He waved and strode off, and Charlie lifted the torn flap of the envelope. Inside was a letter, on official paper headed *Kenworthy's. Est. 1892. A Good Tradition.* It was addressed to Mr Feinstein.

Dear David,

You know perfectly well that I hate schoolchildren. I never let school parties up to the roof garden—most teachers know better than to ask by now. But if it's only one, and if you swear he's an angel, I'll stretch a point this time. Seeing as it's you.

Tell him to come on a weekday afternoon (not Friday). He should ask for me, in person, and if I like the look of him, I'll take him up there. As long as you promise to do Tottie's wedding photographs.

Yours,

Sally

Sarah Marchant—Store Manager.

So Mr Feinstein was still on about that wretched overview? Charlie pushed the letter into his coat pocket. Maybe it was a good idea, but he couldn't concentrate on anything like that. Not until after Wednesday.

'You can't!' Zoë said. 'You can't go off like that today. It's my birthday!'

Charlie stood in the school gateway and stared at her. Wednesday. Of course. The sixth of June. He couldn't believe he hadn't made the connection.

'I suppose you've forgotten my present as well?' Zoë said sulkily.

'Of course I haven't. It's sitting at home, on my desk,' Charlie said. 'I just lost track of the date.'

'Well, you know it now,' said Zoë. 'So you can just forget about that walk. We're going back to your house, the way we always do.'

Rachel smiled nervously, trying to smooth things over. 'Your mum let me peep at the cake yesterday. It's beautiful.'

It was. Charlie had even sat and watched her ice it. A crinoline lady, with a delicate china head and body, handed down from Grandma. And a vast hooped skirt made of cake covered in ornate loops of icing and sugar flowers. He'd seen all that and he simply hadn't realized. For some reason, he'd had it fixed in his mind that Zoë's birthday was on Thursday.

She was grinning now, certain that she'd won. 'We're having a barbecue when Mum and Dad get back from work. Your mother's making the salads, and Mum's got three special gateaux.'

'Great,' Charlie said. His mind was working at top speed. He didn't want to annoy Zoë, but he *had* to go to Toller's Mill, in case Peter turned up. 'Look, Zoë, I must go out for a little bit. But I'll be back in plenty of time for the barbecue. Tell Mum—'

It wasn't going to work. He could see it wasn't going to work. They'd spent their birthdays together ever since Rachel was born. Zoë would have a party for her friends, at the weekend, but the actual birthday was a family day. She'd never let him miss it.

The only thing to do was make a quick getaway.

Charlie lifted his head and looked over Zoë's shoulder. 'Who's that waving to you? Eleanor?'

As Zoë turned round, he began to run. She whirled back, but he was already too far away for her to catch and she yelled after him furiously.

'I know why you're going! There's only one person who could make you miss my birthday. *You're going to meet Peter Luttrell!*'

It had to be a lucky guess, nothing more. But it stopped Charlie in his tracks. He stopped and called back, as cheerfully as he could.

'Don't be a goon! I'm not going to miss anything. I'll be there soon. And—' He suddenly thought of a consolation he could offer her. '—you can go up to my room and find your present. Don't wait for me. The parcel's on my desk.'

He didn't hang about to see whether that calmed her down. He just ran as fast as he could, until he was out of sight.

It was the first time he'd been to the alder pool since Peter gave him the map. As he slid down the bank, his eyes were hunting for secret, hidden details.

Yes, there was a mossy old apple tree on the opposite bank. It was wild and half-dead, but he could see small green apples on the highest branches. And the pool was black and deep. Charlie stared down at it, imagining the powerful, streamlined movements of a hunting otter.

good cover. fish under the bank.

Flopping on to the ground, he lay back and closed his eyes. He could hear the water gurgling in the reedbed, and a late cuckoo calling somewhere upstream. The dry leaves behind him rustled as a bird hopped through them.

And feet sounded in the bushes.

Charlie opened his eyes and sat up. Peter was sitting down beside him, staring across the river. Quite still, except for his moving fingers that picked at a dry twig, stripping off the bark. He was small beside Charlie, and the skin on his hands was pale and thin, stretched tight over the bony knuckles.

'I came to the shed,' Charlie said. 'I saw you.'

Peter nodded. He took two photographs out of his pocket and spread them on his lap. Charlie's first picture, of the long wake trailing across the orange light, and the second one of the otter itself, gazing into the camera with eyes like glass. Focused on some unimaginable, remote reality.

Suddenly, Charlie found it difficult to breathe. He was terrified of asking the wrong question. Peter picked at the twig, with his head bent, and Charlie looked at the otter's face and thought of moving through dark water.

'How do you do it?' he said softly.

'I don't . . . ' Peter pulled off a long strand of bark, twisting it tightly round one finger. His voice was rough and awkward. 'I don't *do* anything. When things get really bad, I just—'

'Change?'

Peter shook his head and let the twist of bark fall away, on to the photographs. It lay in a loose curl, shaped by the pressure of his finger. 'Not change. Go free.'

'Free . . . ' Charlie said.

Ugly words hissed in his head—*familiar, shape-shifter, witch*. The smoke of them drifted across his mind, making him shudder. Was Zoë right? Was it true that he couldn't see what was right under his nose?

Then he remembered what Mr Feinstein always said. What he hammered into them, week after week. *Get out there and use your eyes. Look for yourselves!* He looked.

And he saw Peter. Nervous and alert and strange, but not dangerous. Not evil. And in front of Peter was the river, with its endless, various movement, its dappled shallows and mysterious depths. A whole world of creatures and plants, of shifting temperatures and flowing water. Beautiful and unknowable.

'You know they're trying to catch you?' Charlie said.

Peter nodded and stripped off the last piece of bark. 'The net. They haven't decided where to put it yet.'

Charlie looked down at his fingers. 'Jennifer says—your father can't bear it. That he can't bear having an animal in the garden.'

The twig snapped suddenly. Peter dropped the pieces on to the ground and picked up the photographs. 'Wildness,' he said. 'He doesn't like wildness and things that go free.' He stood up, slipping the pictures into his pocket. 'Come and see.'

Chapter Twenty-Four

Peter began to walk along the bank, without waiting, and Charlie scrambled up to follow. They followed the river through the willow tangles and out into the wide strip of beeches. In silence, they walked over the Old Bridge and headed up River Walk.

As soon as the Luttrells' house came into sight, Charlie could see that the front garden had changed dramatically. The neat flower bed by the boarded gate was churned up and two rose bushes lay with their roots in the air, their bright flowers dusty and trampled. Something had dug a deep trench under the gate, pushing bushes and paving stones out of its way to get into the back garden.

Or out of it.

Charlie stared, imagining the desperate energy it must have taken to dig up all that dry, hard earth.

'You?'

'I had to get out.' The mutter was almost too low for Charlie to hear.

'But why the *front* gate?'

Peter didn't answer. He turned down the alley, leading the way on to the river bank. The whole bank looked oddly bare, but Charlie didn't realize why, until they were almost at the back gate. Then he saw what had been done.

Neat, white-painted boards had been nailed across the gate, making it impossible to open. And all the ground around it had been cleared and concreted over.

'Your father did that?' he said.

Peter nodded. 'It goes all the way.' His voice was tight and unhappy. 'Too far to dig under any more.'

Charlie walked up to the gate and looked over. The concrete continued underneath it and spread out across the garden, as far as the shed. Most of the laurel bushes had been uprooted to make way for it, and a quarter of the lawn had disappeared.

'All that?' Charlie said. 'Because of a bit of digging?'

Peter picked a tall spike of grass and began to shred it with his fingers. 'He's buying more stuff on his way home. To concrete the front.'

'But—' Charlie looked at the bare, ugly concrete. 'What will you do?'

Peter shrugged. 'I don't do anything,' he said.

Charlie wanted to offer some kind of answer, but he couldn't find one. He was still thinking when the kitchen door opened and Mr Luttrell looked out.

'What are you doing, Peter?' he called. 'I've told you before not to play around on the river bank. It's filthy. There's no knowing what you might pick up.'

Even from the other end of the garden, Charlie could tell how tense he was. It was almost unbearable. The sound of that sharp, controlled voice made him want to scream and smash something, just to reduce the pressure. It was like waiting for a thunderstorm. Longing to see the lightning.

The lightning didn't come. Instead, Jennifer scurried out of the house. Before she was half-way down the garden, Peter disappeared along the bank and up the alley, but she didn't turn round. She came right to the gate and gave Charlie a long, steady look.

'Peter brought you to see the concrete?'

Charlie nodded.

'So? What do you think?'

Charlie hunted for words that would be true without hurting her. But there weren't any. 'It's crazy,' he said. 'He's ruined the garden, just to get rid of a few animal footprints.'

Jennifer shrugged. 'You try telling him that.'

'*Have* you tried?'

'Of course. I've tried and Mum has too. But he won't listen. It's an obsession.'

'Don't you think you ought to talk to someone? Outside the family?'

'I don't want to talk to anyone!' Jennifer said fiercely. 'I just want the whole thing to be over. I want the trap to work.'

Charlie looked down, avoiding her eyes. 'Where's he going to put it, then?'

'I don't know yet. But he says he's thought of a wonderful place. Where the thing will slide straight in, before it can stop itself . . . We're going to rig it up tonight, after dark.'

'In the *dark*?' That sounded crazy.

'So no one tries to interfere.' Jennifer's face twisted miserably. 'He's starting to think there must be people involved. Protecting the mink.'

Charlie felt sick. 'Look, he's *ill*. Catching the animal won't solve that. If you really want to help your dad, you ought to make him go to a doctor. And get someone to help him look after his mother.'

'I ought to make him?' Jennifer said. As if Charlie had cracked a particularly silly joke. 'How am I supposed to do that?'

'I don't know, but—'

She was angry now. 'Go away! You don't understand at all!'

'No!' Charlie said. 'Listen—'

He was on the verge of telling her everything, but she didn't give him a chance. Reaching over the gate, she planted a hand in the middle of his chest and shoved him, hard. He staggered backwards, taken by surprise, and almost fell. By the time he had recovered his balance, Jennifer was half-way up the garden, marching stiffly.

Charlie walked back to the alley, wishing she could be right. Wishing that everything could be solved, quite simply, by catching a wild animal in a nylon bag. But he knew that wasn't the solution. He couldn't see any solution at all.

He had forgotten Zoë again. It was only when he got home and saw the balloons tied to the door knocker that he remembered her birthday. He began to walk faster, but as soon as he let himself into the kitchen, he saw that he was too late. The place was deserted, and there was a note from his mother on the kitchen table.

Don't know what happened to you, but we can't wait any longer. You'll have to come and find us at Alison's. Make sure you're in time to eat, and bring a camera.

Drat and double drat. Now there would be a three-star copper-bottomed row. Zoë would be furious and noisy, because he was late. His mother would be furious and upset, because he'd spoilt Zoë's birthday. His father would be angry—quietly and devastatingly—because he had made his mother upset.

And there was absolutely no way of explaining, to any of them, why he hadn't been able to come before. He would have to grovel and apologize and promise never to do it again. And then he would have to take dozens of Jolly Family Snaps, to show what a good time they were all having.

Oh well, he might as well get on with it. He dropped the note into the bin, dumped his bag and went up to change out of his school clothes. As he pushed open his bedroom door, he was vaguely aware of an odd flutter, but he didn't know what it was until he opened his wardrobe door and saw the reflection of Peter's map behind him.

It was ruined.

Someone had scrawled a huge black eye right across the centre, digging in the pen so fiercely that the paper had ripped. An irregular flap hung down over the blue loop of river, fluttering slightly in the draught from the window.

Darting outwards from the eye, in all directions, were jagged black arrows, each one tipped with a blob of dripping red. And across the bottom of the map was a sentence written in rough, hasty capitals.

DESTROY THE EVIL EYE!

Charlie stared at it for a long time, waiting for himself to stop shaking. When he could trust his hands, he peeled the map off the wall and let it roll up on his bed, while he took out his jeans and a T-shirt.

When he had changed, he picked up his camera bag and set off for Alison's. With the map tucked under his arm.

Chapter Twenty-Five

All the way to Alison's, he was rehearsing words in his head. Furious, icy sentences that would make Zoë collapse into floods of tears. But there was no satisfaction in imagining it.

When he got there, they were all out in the back garden. He could hear them laughing and shrieking.

'Zoë, you are a clown!'

'Be careful what you're doing with that fork!'

Charlie walked down the side of the house and stood behind the lilac tree watching Zoë prance round, determinedly enjoying herself. She and Rachel had changed into shorts and T-shirts and they were both barefoot, skipping about behind the barbecues. It looked like a wonderful jolly family party.

It *was* a wonderful jolly party.

Charlie put down the rolled up map and took out his Minolta. One shot, before it was all spoilt. He studied the scene carefully.

There were steaks and chicken joints on the big barbecue, where Zoë was in charge, and Bill had set up the little camping barbecue as well, with a brick under its broken leg. Rachel was behind that, looking after the sausages.

Charlie's mum and dad were sitting next to her, with drinks in their hands, and Bill was busy at the table, laying out salads. When Alison came out of the kitchen with a gateau in each hand, Charlie called out to them all.

'Hey!'

Zoë looked up, flourishing her cook's fork, and Rachel gave him a quick, surprised smile. Charlie took the shot at the perfect moment.

Then Zoë scowled. 'So you finally made it. Didn't *your friend* need you any more?'

'Don't be silly, Zoë. I'm sure Charlie's got a perfectly good reason for being late.' Alison smiled at him.

Charlie knew the smile was a question, but he wasn't going to be distracted. He zipped the camera back into his bag and picked up the map. Deliberately, so that Zoë would realize what it was.

'Oh well,' Bill said, with heavy cheerfulness. 'Better late than never. Let's get on with the party, shall we?'

'No,' Charlie said.

They all stared at him, and Bill blinked. 'What?'

'I don't want a party,' Charlie said. 'I don't want to celebrate Zoë's birthday.'

Rachel looked horrified, but Zoë's face didn't change. She knew why not.

Charlie's mother put her drink down. 'Don't quarrel now,' she said quickly. 'Not this evening. Whatever it is, it can wait.'

'No, it can't,' Charlie said. 'How can I wish Zoë a happy birthday when she's just vandalized this?' He held the map up, without unrolling it.

'I didn't,' Zoë said. Too fast. 'And anyway, it's just a load of scribble.'

'Oh, Zoë—' Alison said.

Just as Charlie's mother said, 'I'm sure there's a reasonable explanation—'

They stopped, as though they'd bumped into each other, and Charlie spoke into the silence. 'There's an explanation all right. She ruined it because Peter Luttrell made it. She's spent the whole year picking on him. Because she's got some silly idea that he has magic powers.'

Rachel gave a strange squeak and looked down at her rickety barbecue. Zoë prodded at the steak on hers.

'Oh, Zoë,' Alison said again, in quite a different voice. Amused and exasperated. 'Magic?'

'He's making it up,' Zoë said stiffly. 'I don't know what he's talking about. I don't believe in magic.'

'That's right!' Charlie's voice was silky. 'You don't, do you?'

Zoë looked across at him, uncertain of what he meant. It was all he could do not to grin. Slowly, he walked towards her, holding up the map.

'If you really believed in magic, you wouldn't have dared to scribble on this. You'd have been much too afraid of . . . *the Evil Eye*!'

In one, swift movement, he unrolled the map, pushing it forward so that the scrawled eye was staring straight at Zoë, just a few inches from her face.

He only meant to startle her. But, as the eye uncoiled, Rachel went pale and stepped back. Zoë caught her breath and snatched at the map, tweaking it out of Charlie's hands. As she grabbed it, the paper rolled up again.

'Careful!' Charlie shouted.

He was too late. Zoë whisked the map away and the long white roll knocked against the little camping barbecue, toppling it off its wobbly legs. It fell towards Rachel and she jumped back, but not far enough. The barbecue fell against her left leg, and hot charcoal showered out, on to her bare foot.

There was a split second of appalling silence, and then Rachel began to scream.

* * *

Everyone moved fast. Bill grabbed a jug of fruit juice from the table and tipped it over Rachel's foot, Alison pushed Zoë aside and began knocking away the charcoal with her bare hands, and Charlie's father raced into the kitchen.

He was back in a couple of moments, with two large bags of frozen peas. 'Put these round her foot while we drive her to hospital. I'll take my car.'

By the time Bill had carried Rachel round, the car was started and backed out into the road. Rachel had stopped screaming now. She lolled against the back seat with her eyes closed and her face deathly pale. Bill was supporting her with one arm, and Alison slid in on her other side.

'Hurry!' she said. '*Get going!*'

The car drew away, and Charlie's mother walked back into the garden. She smiled at Charlie and Zoë. A shaky smile.

'Let's not panic until we know whether there's something to worry about. I'll go and put the kettle on, shall I?'

Zoë was sitting on the grass, with her head in her hands. She nodded, without looking up, as Mrs Willcox disappeared into the kitchen. Suddenly Charlie felt very sorry for her. He went across and put a hand on her shoulder.

'Don't worry. Accidents happen. She'll be OK.'

Zoë shrank away from his fingers. 'Accidents?' she said. Her voice was muffled by her hands.

'Don't be like that,' Charlie said gently. 'It wasn't your fault.'

'Of course it wasn't my fault.' Zoë lifted her head. Charlie had thought she was crying, but there were no tears. Her face was grim and set. 'What are you talking about?'

'I just meant you shouldn't blame yourself,' Charlie said. 'Everyone knows you didn't do it on purpose.'

Zoë gave him a sharp, scornful look that he didn't understand, but she didn't say anything else, because Mrs Willcox came out again.

'Poor Zoë,' she said. 'This is a rotten birthday for you. Look, why don't we eat that steak? It's silly to waste it, and we can do some more for the others when they get back.'

But when the car came back from the hospital, Rachel wasn't in it.

'She's going to be fine,' Alison said. Brightly. 'They said we'd done brilliant first aid, but the burns are quite bad and she's very shocked. The doctor kept her in overnight, for observation.'

She made them go on with the barbecue, but it was a sad, subdued affair. Charlie's father took charge of the cooking and Bill made twice as many terrible jokes as usual, but they were all play-acting. In the end, Alison and Charlie's mother gave up the pretence. They drew their chairs together, talking in low voices, and when Charlie and Zoë were collecting the plates, they caught a snatch of the conversation.

' . . . can't understand why she's so shaken,' Alison was saying. ' . . . she usually bounces back . . . the doctor says it's just shock, but I'm surprised . . . '

Zoë's eyes flickered, but she didn't speak. Not until she and Charlie were alone in the kitchen, loading the dishwasher. Then she muttered savagely as she threw the knives and forks into the cutlery basket.

'*I'm* not surprised Rachel's shocked. I bet *she* knows what's happened to her.'

'What do you mean?' Charlie said.

Zoë gave a noisy, impatient sigh. 'You're still ignoring it, aren't you? Even when it's right under your nose.' Her face was ferocious.

Charlie scraped the plates into the bin. 'I don't see what there is to see.'

'You've forgotten what was on Peter's table. That day we went round to his house.'

'Peter's table . . .?' For a moment, Charlie couldn't think what she was talking about. Then he remembered, with a sick jolt.

'That's right!' Zoë said. 'That figure. It must have been a model of Rachel. *The leg was damaged.*'

Charlie felt the world spin. 'Don't be silly!'

'I'm not being silly.' Zoë began throwing plates into the dishwasher. 'You've only got to look at the facts. That model had no foot, and Rachel's burnt her foot. What more proof do you want?' She stood up suddenly, peering into Charlie's face. 'Can you put your hand on your heart and say there's nothing peculiar about Peter Luttrell?'

Charlie hesitated. He couldn't help it. That was enough for Zoë. She stepped back and folded her arms.

'You see?'

'Peter didn't make that barbecue fall on Rachel's foot,' Charlie said, as firmly and clearly as he knew how. 'You did. You didn't mean to, but you knocked it over with the map.'

'And who made the map?' Zoë said triumphantly.

It was nonsense. Charlie knew it was nonsense. But he couldn't see how to convince Zoë. She was clicking pieces together, like someone doing a mad jigsaw puzzle.

She gave him a moment to agree with her and when he didn't she leaned forward and hissed, 'He's injured Rachel and he's got you in his power, but we're not going to let him get away with it. We're going to prove what he is, and make him stop!'

Chapter Twenty-Six

Charlie felt he'd stepped into a nightmare. And it hadn't gone away when he woke up the next morning. Rachel was still in hospital, and Zoë's voice was humming in his brain. *We're not going to let him get away with it. We're going to prove what he is, and make him stop!* He didn't know where to start worrying.

'You look really ropy,' his mother said, sticking her head in on her way to work. 'Want to stay at home today?'

He did—but he knew that he couldn't. He couldn't stay at home while Zoë went to school. She was as dangerous as a bare electric cable.

'I'm fine.' He managed a grin and a wave, to keep his mother happy, and then struggled out of bed and trailed downstairs to have breakfast with his father.

He meant to talk to him, and tell him some of the truth while they both sat over their toast. But as he was cutting the bread, Alison phoned, and that took all his father's attention.

'That's not bad news,' he kept saying, soothingly. 'She's going to be fine, Alison. It wasn't your fault. Yes, it makes sense to throw that old barbecue away, but you mustn't blame yourself.'

He was still saying the same things, patiently and reassuringly, when Charlie left for school.

The day was a torment. Charlie had gone in with all sorts of good intentions. He was going to take Zoë aside and talk to her, reasonably and calmly. He was going to tell her that her parents could do without any more hassle. That, whatever she thought about Peter, she mustn't rock the boat for the time being.

But he didn't get a chance. Zoë was never on her own. Whenever he saw her, she had her arm linked through Eleanor's, and the two of them were whispering savagely. And the moment they caught sight of him, they glared and spun away. Once they even ran off to make sure that he wouldn't catch up.

At lunch time, he lost them altogether. He walked round and round, inside the building and outside, asking people where they were. He knew that he sounded too anxious, because of the odd looks that people were giving him, but he didn't care. The more he didn't find them, the more dangerous they seemed.

It was only as the bell was ringing that someone told him they were in the library. He hadn't got time to walk round to the entrance, but he ran and looked through the window— and there they were. Sitting side by side in front of the CD-Rom reader, with their heads together. Eleanor was pointing at something on the screen, tapping the glass with a gleeful finger.

Charlie waited for her to move out of the way, so that he could see what she was looking at, but she didn't. Instead, she glanced over her shoulder and saw him staring. Instantly, her hand darted to the keyboard and the picture snapped back to the main menu. Then she and Zoë whisked off, out of the library.

Something was going to happen. Charlie knew it. But there was nothing he could do for the moment. The two of them would be safely in class before he was even in the building. He'd have to make sure that he caught Zoë at the end of school.

He tried hard. Five minutes after the bell rang, he was at the school gate, waiting for Zoë to appear. He was quite prepared to make a fool of himself by racing after her if she ran off.

But he hadn't spotted Alison, waiting along the road with the car. Zoë appeared with Eleanor and they both whipped straight past him and jumped into it. Charlie was left standing at the gate, gazing after them. He didn't even know whether Zoë was going home or not.

There was only one thing he could do. Spinning round, he raced back into school, ignoring the way people stared. He ran all the way along the back corridor and flung the library door open.

Mrs Ramm looked up from the computer and raised her eyebrows. 'Is there something you want?'

'Zoë?' Charlie said.

Mrs Ramm didn't pretend not to understand. She looked grave. 'She was in here at lunch time, with Eleanor Martin. Asking for books about witches, and looking very . . . excited.'

Charlie closed his eyes and his brain swirled.

'Is there anything you want to tell me?' Mrs Ramm said.

Her voice cut through the turmoil, very cool and clear, and Charlie opened his eyes and looked up at her.

'I'm afraid—' How could he explain, even to her? He didn't know how to begin. 'I've got to *find* them. Do you know where they've gone?'

Mrs Ramm shook her head slowly. 'They were talking about the river when they left, but that's no help. Unless you know something I don't know. Has Zoë got a special bit of river? Somewhere she always goes?'

Charlie frowned. 'Not that I know of. It could be anywhere. I could work my way along it, I suppose.'

'Too slow,' Mrs Ramm said, gently. 'You'd need a helicopter.'

Charlie nodded, ruefully, pushing his hands into his pockets. Picking at the paper in the right hand pocket of his jacket. 'I'll have to see if her mother knows where she's gone.' He knew she wouldn't have told Alison, but at least that would be something to do. 'Maybe I'm being neurotic.' His fingers twisted the paper, rolling one corner of the—

The envelope.

Suddenly, he realized what it was that he was fiddling with. Pushing a hand into his pocket, he pulled out the envelope, remembering what Mr Feinstein had said in the café. . . . *it's even better from the roof garden. Up there, you can see right round to the sewage works. And all along the back of River Walk, as well . . .*

He could get that overview that Mr Feinstein was always nagging him about. He could see the whole river at once. All he needed was the right equipment.

He picked up his bag. 'It's all right,' he gabbled. 'I've got an idea.' He was half-way to the door when Mrs Ramm called after him.

'Wait a minute!'

She followed very fast, almost running.

'I don't want to pry. But if there's trouble, and you need help—' She picked up the notepad from her desk and scribbled a number on the top sheet. 'This is where I am, when I'm not at school. You can phone any time.'

Charlie didn't see what she could do, but he felt comforted. He took the piece of paper and slipped it into his pocket. 'Thanks.'

Then he headed for home, as fast as he could, to fetch his cameras.

* * *

Up on Kenworthy's roof, the roses were blooming.

'And I don't want you picking them,' Sally Marchant said. She was short and brisk and very much in charge. 'Or flinging yourself over the parapet. Or sniffing glue.'

'I'm going to take photographs,' Charlie said meekly. 'If that's all right.' He breathed in the hot, heavy scent of the roses and wished that was the whole truth.

'I don't suppose you can do much harm with a camera.' Sally Marchant didn't exactly smile, but she looked at him as if he were a human being after all. 'Want to get started?'

'Yes,' Charlie said. 'Thanks.' Shouldering his bag, he climbed the raised terrace in the centre of the garden.

He was expecting a view like the one from the café. He hadn't realized quite what a difference it would make, being right on top. Once his head was above the level of the parapet, he could see the full loop of the river, from the alder pool right round to the sewage works. It was like seeing Peter's map come to life.

But there was no sign of Zoë and Eleanor.

'What sort of pictures are you planning on taking?' Sally Marchant said.

Until that moment, Charlie hadn't given it a thought, but he had to give her an answer. And suddenly he knew what he would have wanted. If he'd really been concentrating on the pictures.

'I'm going to make a panorama. If I take a sequence of pictures, turning the camera bit by bit, I can fit them together into a circle, to show how the river curls around the town.'

'Sounds good.' She looked impressed. 'Let's see how you do it.'

Charlie wished he hadn't been so clever. He didn't want her to stay. He wanted her to go back to her office and leave him to hunt for Zoë, but he couldn't say that. Smiling politely, he set up his tripod and prepared the camera. Then he began to work his way clockwise along the curve of the river, taking photographs slowly and systematically.

First the wide, open stretch, where the river straightened and then flowed away to the sea, past the estate where he lived and the sewage works that squatted like a toad on the far side.

sewage outflow. foul water and no fish.

Then the Jubilee Walkway, and the castle ruins, where the river had been built up into a defence.

slimy walls. no way to land.

Three more shots took him past the New Bridge and round to the school. For the first time, he realized how the old hedgerow ran in a dense strip from the school library down one side of the games field and round the back of the sports centre. All the way to the river.

The otter must have taken that route to the river, the day Peter blanked out in the library. Charlie imagined the long brown body hunching and straightening as it ran, and then plunging in and swimming upstream, past the New Bridge and Toller's Mill. To the alder pool.

As he followed its path, moving the tripod round to photograph the Old Bridge, he began thinking about the alder pool. He had to have a picture of that, but it would mean shooting straight into the sun. He glanced up.

'I'm afraid it's getting cloudy,' Sally Marchant said, not understanding.

Charlie shook his head, vaguely, watching the little cloud that was inching its way across the sky. 'No, that's good. I think I'll wait for the cloud.'

'Please yourself. It's time I went and did some work. Come and let me know when you've finished.'

She headed for the door and rattled away downstairs. Charlie watched the cloud drift right across the sun. Then he took hold of the tripod, to turn it, and looked down into the viewfinder.

And he saw something that stopped him dead.

Three tiny figures were coming through the strip of woodland between Kenworthy's and the river. They were close under the back wall of Kenworthy's yard and from the ground they would have been invisible, but he could see them clearly. It was Zoë and Eleanor.

And Peter.

They were dragging him along, and whenever he tried to stop, they jerked his arms up painfully behind him, forcing him forwards. For a moment, Charlie couldn't understand why Peter wasn't yelling for help. Then he saw the blue gag across his mouth, and the scarf ends trailing down his back.

Zoë had done that? *Zoë?*

Charlie leaned forward, watching as they dragged Peter on, past Kenworthy's to the fallen willow trees. With a combination of tugging and bullying, they got him over the trunks, into the wilder patch of woodland beyond. There, they were screened from the houses on the other bank, in River Walk. No one at all could see them, except Charlie.

When they were half-way to Toller's Mill, they stopped. Zoë began to talk at Peter. Charlie couldn't hear the words, but he knew, from the way she was wagging her head, that it was some kind of lecture. Every now and again, she stopped expectantly, as though she had asked a question. And Peter shook his head hard.

Then Eleanor took a cord out of her pocket.

Even then, Charlie didn't realize what was going on. Not until Eleanor tied Peter's hands behind his back and ran the cord down to knot his ankles together. When he was completely tied up, she and Zoë started to drag him towards the river. He struggled to hold back, but Eleanor simply lifted his tied feet off the ground, so that she and Zoë were carrying him.

And he went rigid.

Even from where he was, Charlie saw that stiffening. Zoë stopped uncertainly, but Eleanor shook Peter's feet and Charlie caught the rise of her voice as she shouted at him. She dragged Zoë on impatiently, to the very edge of the river.

For a moment they stood there, talking to each other across Peter's motionless body. They were so absorbed in what they were saying that they didn't see what was happening in the thicket just beyond them.

But Charlie did. He saw a low, brown body slide out of a patch of nettles beside the river.

It slipped down the bank and into the water with hardly a ripple. If he hadn't known it was there, he would never have noticed the top of its head as it worked its way downstream, in among the reeds.

The otter.

The otter that was full of life while Peter lay motionless and unconscious.

Suddenly, Charlie was icy with fear. He yelled down, as loudly as he could. 'Zoë! Stop it!'

She couldn't have made out the words, but she must have caught some kind of sound. Charlie saw her face as she turned, and he yelled again, so hard that he thought his lungs would burst.

'You'll kill him!'

Zoë's eyes scanned the back of Kenworthy's, her head tilting as she looked up, trying to work out where the sound had come from. Charlie was just taking a long breath, ready to yell again, when she saw him. Even at that distance, she obviously knew who it was.

'Zoë!' he shouted.

She turned away, deliberately, and said something to Eleanor. Then the two of them began to swing Peter's body.

Abandoning all his equipment, Charlie scrambled down the terrace steps, towards the door. He pulled the bolt open, so fast that he skinned his knuckles, and rattled down the stairs at top speed.

There was no time to wait for the lift. When he came out by the café entrance, he just raced for the next flight of stairs, knocking old ladies out of the way.

As he reached the third floor, he saw Sally Marchant talking to someone by the counter. She turned at the clatter of his feet and her mouth opened, but he didn't wait to hear what she was going to say. By the time any sound was out, he was on the second floor, and heading for the first.

He stumbled off the stairs when he reached the ground floor, and fell through the revolving doors into the street. Then he raced down the side of the building, with his breath coming in great, painful gasps, and slithered down the side of the Old Bridge, into the woods.

He had forgotten that it was so far to the fallen willow trees. His feet skidded on the loose ground under the beeches and his chest was hurting, but he forced himself on, clambering over the willow trunks without noticing how the branches scratched him.

As he pushed his way through the tangle beyond, he was shouting again, even though he had no breath left. 'Zoë! Stop!'

In between shouts, he was listening, desperately, for the sound of a splash. But he must have missed it, because when he came through the bushes Zoë and Eleanor were alone on the river bank.

With his last shreds of strength, he yelled at them both. 'Where is he? What have you done with him?'

Zoë's face was white. 'He should have floated!' she said angrily. 'Witches are supposed to float!'

Then her face crumpled, and she started to cry.

Chapter Twenty-Seven

Charlie was beyond speaking. He leaned against a tree, to hold himself up, and pointed at the river, and Zoë kicked off her trainers and went in without a word. She waded out a few feet from the bank and then disappeared under the surface of the murky water.

'How long has he been in there?' Charlie gasped, when he had enough breath.

Eleanor shrugged, turning her head away. Her face was blank, disowning everything. Charlie pushed her away and knelt down on the bank, waiting for Zoë to surface.

It seemed a terrifyingly long time, but it couldn't have been more than a few seconds. Her head reappeared, streaming water, and she rolled on to her back, dragging Peter up with an arm round his chest.

'Heavy!' she panted.

Peter's eyes were closed and his face lolled sideways towards the bank. Charlie anchored himself with one arm round a willow and leaned out as far as he could.

'Can you get any closer?'

Zoë kicked frantically, and Charlie reached out an inch more and grabbed hold of the cord that tied Peter's hands, hauling the two of them in. As they slithered against the bank, he yelled to Eleanor.

'Don't just stand there! Come and help!'

She came, sullenly, and the three of them struggled together. Peter's clothes were sodden and his shoes were full of water, and it took all their energy to lift him.

'Well done, Zoë,' Charlie panted, as they finally tugged him on to the bank.

'Is he breathing?' Zoë said.

Her voice was sharp and anxious. Clambering up after Peter, she knelt beside him and began to unknot the gag, tugging at the wet wool with frantic fingers. When she finally managed to untie it, she pulled his jaw down, scooping out a long strand of slimy weed. Charlie struggled with the cord, wrenching it off Peter's wrists and ankles.

Peter's face was smeared with mud and there was a scratch down one cheek. Zoë wiped his lips with the back of her hand. Then she took a breath and pressed her mouth down over his.

Charlie breathed with her, watching Peter's chest rise and fall. One. Two. Three. Four. Then a rest, and then again. One, two, three, four.

When Zoë lifted her head for the second time, she said, 'Eleanor . . . go for an ambulance.'

Eleanor scowled. 'That's going to mean trouble. Can't we wait and see—?'

'Wait and see?' Zoë's face twisted in disgust. 'Don't you understand? We may have killed him! We were completely wrong about everything. Just call the ambulance!'

She lowered her head again, and Charlie fumbled in his pocket. 'Get to the phone box as fast as you can,' he said. 'And . . . here.' He pulled out Mrs Ramm's piece of paper. 'Phone this number and tell her to come. Say it's Peter.'

He thrust the paper into Eleanor's hand and gave her a push that sent her staggering towards the bushes. In a couple of paces she had disappeared, but they could still hear her as she clawed her way over the willow trunks and broke into a run on the other side.

Zoë lifted her head again. 'It's not going to work,' she said miserably. 'He won't breathe at all. He's gone.'

'Keep trying!' Charlie said.

The word she had used echoed in his mind. Gone. He picked up the cord and the scarf and stood up, twisting them in his hands as he looked downstream.

There was no sign of the otter. He could see all the way to the curve of the river, just before the Luttrells' house, and there was nothing to disturb the smooth, shining water. No rippling, V-shaped wake. No dark head, breaking the surface with its uptilted nostrils.

Gone.

He looked back, watching the dip and rise of Zoë's head. One, two, three, four. She was working steadily, blowing air into Peter's lungs with utter concentration. Doing it perfectly, the way she'd been taught in her first aid classes. Charlie wondered how long she could keep it up, and whether he ought to take a turn.

He was just going to offer, when he heard the otter whistle.

It came from downstream. The same shrill sound that he'd heard in the garden. And it didn't sound very far away. He put a hand on Zoë's shoulder.

'I've got to go for a minute—'

She flashed him one startled look as she lifted her head. Then she nodded and bent over Peter again. Charlie tossed away the cord and the scarf, into the bushes, and began to run back along the bank, listening for another whistle, as he pushed his way through the thicket.

He didn't hear it. Instead, as he reached the fallen willows, there was a yell from across the river. From the direction of the Luttrells' house. A man's voice, distorted with fury.

'Come back, you—!'

Charlie threw himself at the willow trunks, catching his foot in a cluster of new branches sprouting on top. He sprawled headlong, with his hands on the ground and his feet in the air.

Trapped like that, he saw Mr Luttrell come charging into the alley, brandishing a cricket bat in his hand. And ahead of him, racing for the bank with a humped, lolloping run, was the otter.

It reached the river while he was still only half-way down the alley. Charlie saw it go head first down the mud slide, its body streamlined, aiming for the water. It vanished under the surface as Mr Luttrell ran out on to the bank.

He was in a frenzy, red-faced and panting. The hair that disguised his bald patch was hanging in long strands over one ear, and his eyes were glaring at the river.

He caught sight of Charlie, still struggling to free his leg, and bellowed at him. 'Where did that thing go into the water?' He rocked on the balls of his feet, nursing the cricket bat.

Charlie scrambled up. 'Never mind that! You've got to come with me. Peter—'

'Shut up!' Mr Luttrell snapped, not taking his eyes off the water. 'That can wait. I'm going to catch this wretched mink. It came right up to the house and peered in at me!'

'But Peter—' Charlie began, despairingly.

And then he realized that he didn't have to make Mr Luttrell listen. Because, when the otter surfaced out in midstream, he would follow it, and it would lead him to Peter. That was why it had come. Charlie turned and looked across the water, waiting for the little dark head to bob up.

But it didn't bob up. Instead, the water by the Luttrells' bank began to boil and churn, as if a great hand were stirring it from underneath.

'Where did it go in?' Mr Luttrell called again, insistently.

'Down the mud slide,' Charlie said. 'Why . . . ?'

Mr Luttrell didn't answer, but a slow, ugly smile spread over his face as he stared down at the brown cloud of silt spreading outwards from the bank. At the silver bubbles streaming up in the centre of the whirlpool. He knelt down to peer into the water, putting his hands on the edge of the bank. One on each side of the great brown streak where the mud was worn bare.

And suddenly, looking across at him, Charlie understood.

He's thought of a wonderful place, Jennifer had said. When he wouldn't stop and listen to her. *Where the thing will slide straight in, before it can stop itself . . .*

With sick certainty, Charlie knew that the net was at the bottom of the mud slide. The otter had shot straight down into it. It wasn't coming up, because it was tangled in a bag of strong nylon net.

And it was drowning.

It couldn't breathe water, any more than Peter could. After three or four minutes under the surface, it needed to come up for air. But now it couldn't do that, because it was trapped.

Charlie didn't give himself a chance to think how long it had been down there. Pulling off his shoes and T-shirt, he slid straight down the bank on his side, into the water. His feet hit the soft, muddy bottom and he pulled with his arms, swimming away hard, before the mud could suck him in.

As he headed towards the opposite bank, he heard Mr Luttrell yell at him, but he didn't take in the words. He was too busy trying to remember what the map had said about this piece of the river.

deep water. mud slide. overhanging banks.

From half-way across, he could feel the whirling force of the otter's struggle. He took a deep breath and ducked his head under the surface, forcing his eyes open. The water was as thick as soup. Silt and grit swirled all round him and just ahead, at the heart of the whirlpool, was a denser cloud that he couldn't see into.

He surfaced once, to gulp air, and then went under again, heading straight for that cloud, with his hands outstretched. His eyes were useless now, but his skin guided him. He could feel where the otter was from the way the water thrashed against his face, and he navigated by touch, reaching out into the storm.

His fingers tangled in the net and for a second, between the strands, he felt sleek, resilient hair and a solid, writhing body.

Then the otter turned its head and bit him.

It wasn't like Peter's bite, which had left purple bruises on his knuckles. It was the serious, savage bite of a hunter. Charlie felt strong teeth sink into his flesh. Felt his bones crunch as the powerful muscles clamped together.

All his instincts told him to wrench his hand free and escape. But the otter's frantic struggles were slowing down. He could feel the river settling round him, and he knew that there was no time for second chances. If he abandoned the otter now, it would die.

With his free hand, Charlie groped for the top of the net. Somewhere near the top, there must be an opening. He had to find that.

The otter writhed, with its teeth still clamped, twisting his bones. But he wasn't going to give in. He fumbled with a loose stake that must have held the trap open, and reached beyond it, into a space, with no mesh.

He and the otter were both at the end of their strength. As Charlie's arm dived into the bag, grabbing a fold of skin and thick fur, the fierce jaws opened, letting his other hand go free. With a last effort, the otter strained upwards, towards the air. But its claws were still tangled in the tough net, and it was anchored to the bank, trapped under the overhanging edge.

Charlie's lungs were bursting, but he fumbled at the net with his wounded hand. As the otter's claws came free, he felt its whole body go limp in his arms, and the turmoil in his mind resolved itself into a single, simple word.

Air.

He didn't know, any longer, whose life he was fighting for. He just wrapped both his arms round the otter, hugging it tight to his chest. Then he kicked upwards and they surfaced together, both almost unconscious.

'Filthy thing!' said Mr Luttrell's voice, above his head.

Tilting his head back, Charlie saw his thin, frenzied face staring down, the mouth twisted with anger and the eyes fanatical.

And he saw the outline of the cricket bat, poised in mid air.

'Out of the way!' yelled the voice. Not recognizable now. Pure fury and hatred.

'You . . . can't . . .'

Charlie couldn't speak. His body was too busy sucking in oxygen, taking long, shuddering breaths that he couldn't stop or control. But there was no time to wait. The cricket bat was coming down, straight on to the otter's head.

. . . their skulls are exceptionally fragile . . .

If he let the otter go, it would sink and drown. If he held it above water, it would be battered to death.

Charlie did the only thing that could save it. Still clutching its body, he twisted round, shielding its head with his own. He heard the bat come whistling down through the air, too fast for Mr Luttrell to stop. In the last instant of consciousness, he felt the otter move in his hands, live and muscular as it twisted away into the water.

Then the wood crashed on to his head, knocking him into darkness.

Chapter Twenty-Eight

He was in deep water, falling, falling, with the smell of it in his nostrils, and the taste of it in the back of his throat, falling down and down into green shadows. The water moved against his face, and weed looped his body, as he sank into a dim, alien world.

The light seeped strangely from above, filtered through a haze of tiny particles, growing brighter and fuller and richer. He felt his body relax and spread. He felt his blood drifting into the warm, soft water. Air streamed out of him in a plume of silver bubbles erupting to the surface. A fountain of life, bursting up towards the swelling light.

The beautiful light. The beautiful, beautiful river.

He opened his mouth to the water . . .

And then hard fingers grabbed him. Rough, strong hands dragged his body up, out of the water into harsh air and a man's voice dinned in his ears.

'You little fool!'

Darkness yawned round him. *No*, said his mind. No to the dry air. No to the raw light. No to the wind on his face and the coarse, unfiltered sound and the battering voice.

'You stupid, interfering fool!'

And then his lungs gulped a breath and his eyes opened.

Mr Luttrell was kneeling beside him, staring down with grim, pale eyes. 'What were you doing?' he bellowed. His voice rose, out of control. 'You let it go!'

'I . . . had to. If you kill it—' Charlie was choking, and fighting for breath. 'If you kill it . . . you're killing Peter.'

The words scorched the air between them. For a split second, Mr Luttrell stared, and then his face twisted and his hands shot out. Dragging Charlie's shoulders off the ground, he began to shake him. Shake and shake, as if he would never stop. As if he *could* never stop.

'No!' Charlie yelled.

Mr Luttrell began to yell too, but the words were indistinguishable, lost in the deafening bellow of his voice. His hands gripped and shook, so that Charlie felt his neck was going to break. So that his mouth opened and he started to scream. On and on and on—

'No! No! No!—'

Until a voice sliced through the bellowing and the shaking and the screaming. A calm, commanding voice.

'Stop that at once!' said Mrs Ramm.

Mr Luttrell snatched his hands away, looking down at them as if he couldn't believe what they had just been doing. And Charlie lurched over sideways and was sick, spewing the thick, green river water out of his body.

Mrs Ramm came out of the alley towards them. 'What's going on? Are you all right, Charlie?'

Charlie nodded, shakily. Her eyes travelled to the ragged, blood-stained wound on his hand.

'Don't worry about that,' he said hoarsely. The words rasped his throat. 'It's not . . . me you want to worry about. It's Peter . . . '

Mrs Ramm gave him a sharp look. 'That's what Eleanor Martin said. She phoned me up, and she wouldn't say anything except, *It's Peter.* Where is Peter?'

'Further up the river.' Charlie rolled over on to his knees and heaved himself up with his uninjured hand. 'He—'

There wasn't time to force the words out. A blue light flashed on the opposite bank and the noise of a siren came screeching over the water as the ambulance drove off the road and on to the path under the beech trees. Mrs Ramm understood instantly.

'Quick! My car!' She bent and prodded Mr Luttrell's shoulder. 'Get a move on. You're coming too, aren't you?'

He didn't answer, but he stumbled to his feet and followed them up the alley like a man in a trance.

By the time they reached the car, Charlie was shivering. Mrs Ramm opened the boot and tossed him a blanket. 'Wrap up in that, until we can get you something dry to wear.'

Huddling the blanket round him, Charlie slid on to the back seat, leaning his aching head against the window. Mr Luttrell climbed in, in front of him, and Mrs Ramm ran round to the other side, starting the engine before she had properly closed her door.

She drove fast, in silence, concentrating on getting over the bridge to the other bank of the river. Taking the same track as the ambulance driver had, she swung the car off the road, on to the bare ground under the trees. When they reached the fallen willows, she drew up beside the ambulance.

At that moment, the willow branches in front of them were pulled aside. Zoë struggled over the tree trunks. She turned and held the branches out of the way, so that the men could carry the stretcher through.

Mrs Ramm jumped out of the car and ran towards them. Charlie had opened the door to follow, when he realized that Mr Luttrell wasn't moving. He was sitting absolutely still, staring straight ahead.

'Are you just going to sit there?' Charlie said angrily. 'Don't you want to know if he's alive?'

There was no reply.

Charlie climbed out of the car, and looked in through the front window. Mr Luttrell was staring through the windscreen at the pale shape on the stretcher. Staring and staring, with clenched fists and a tense unhappy face. As if he were afraid to move, in case he exploded.

Charlie wanted to ignore him and run over to the stretcher. He had never wanted to get away from anyone so much, in all his life. But he made himself speak.

'Don't you care? Don't you care about Peter at all?'

'I don't understand—' Mr Luttrell said the words almost without moving his lips. Without taking his eyes off the stretcher.

'What is there to understand?' Charlie said fiercely. 'Peter's there. And he may be dead.'

The men from the ambulance were just lifting the far end of the stretcher carefully over the trunks. Peter was strapped into place, very still and white. His eyes were closed, and the lashes were wet and dark above the sharp angles of his cheekbones.

Mr Luttrell gazed across the space at him. 'I don't understand about . . . that animal.' His voice was low and struggling. 'Why did it look through my window? Why did it come to *me*?'

'Where else would it go?' Charlie's whole body was shaking, but he had to say what was in his head. 'You want everything locked up tight, don't you? So you can keep going. But people can't live like that. If you go on locking Peter out, he'll die.'

Mr Luttrell's tongue flicked over his thin, dry lips. 'It's not so easy—'

'Who cares if it's easy? You're Peter's *father*. No one else will do! You have to open the door and let things happen.'

Charlie swung away from the car and walked over to the willow trees, dragging the blanket tighter round his shoulders. Zoë was still holding the branches as the last man climbed over the tree trunks. Charlie went to stand beside her, looking down at Peter's face on the stretcher.

'Is he . . . ?'

'He's breathing,' Zoë said. Her voice was thick with exhaustion. She let go of the branches and stepped back, rubbing a hand across her face. 'It took a long time, but he started in the end.' She staggered slightly, and Charlie put an arm tight round her shoulders, so that she didn't fall.

That was when Mr Luttrell got out of the car.

He walked up to the stretcher, and the men stood holding it as he looked down.

'Peter?' he said.

Peter's eyes flickered open, and he stiffened.

'It's all right,' Mr Luttrell said. His voice cracked, but he kept on speaking. 'Everything's going to be all right.'

He reached out for the limp hand that was lying on the edge of the stretcher, but Peter flinched, drawing it away sharply. His eyes widened in a steady, unblinking stare. Strange and remote.

'No,' Charlie muttered, under his breath. '*No!*'

He glanced at Mr Luttrell, expecting his face to freeze. Expecting him to snatch his hand back and turn away from the stretcher.

But he didn't. He left the hand lying where it was and he stared back into Peter's distant, glassy eyes, meeting that unnerving gaze. Not turning away, even when the tears started rolling down his face, streaking his smooth-shaved cheeks and seeping into his immaculate, snow-white collar.

Peter's eyes changed, and he blinked. With a great effort, as if he were coming out of some distant place, he focused on his father's face. Very slowly, he moved his hand back to the edge of the stretcher, and Mr Luttrell's fingers closed round it. Then the men began to walk and, still holding Peter's hand, Mr Luttrell went with them, up the steps and into the back of the ambulance.

Mrs Ramm stood watching the ambulance as it bumped away across the uneven ground towards the road. Then she took out her car keys.

'No point in hanging around here,' she said abruptly. 'It's time a doctor had a look at Charlie's hand.'

'What's wrong with his hand?' Zoë said.

Charlie pulled it out of the blanket. It was swelling, and beginning to bleed again. 'I got bitten by an otter.'

'Don't be silly,' Zoë said. 'There aren't any otters in this river.'

Charlie didn't bother to argue. It didn't matter now. He didn't think he would ever see the otter again.

'Two drownings in one day,' Mr Feinstein said. 'And no picture? Call yourself a photographer?'

'No one was drowned,' Charlie said. He lay back against the cushions and grinned. 'Anyway, I had concussion, and there was a bit of trouble with my hand, too. You try pressing buttons when you've been chewed.'

The operation had taken two hours, and the white, bandaged lump didn't seem to have much to do with the rest of his arm.

'You could have used your left hand,' Mr Feinstein said unsympathetically. 'If you were really dedicated.' He grinned back and sat down opposite Charlie, on the sofa. 'I've been to Kenworthy's. Sally Marchant gave me your camera bag—

once she'd finished complaining—so I got the films developed.'

'That's great,' Charlie said. 'Thanks. I'm sorry about Mrs Marchant.' He had a vague memory of her disbelieving, outraged face. 'I had to do something, in a hurry.'

'I heard,' Mr Feinstein said. 'And I'm the one who ought to apologize. If I'd listened to you properly, that day in the café, maybe we could have got things sorted out much sooner. Organized some help for Mr Luttrell and his mother. Before he got so worked up.'

'Well . . . maybe.' Charlie didn't think Mr Luttrell would have accepted help before. He held out his hands for the photographs.

'I haven't looked at them,' Mr Feinstein said. 'I thought you ought to be the first.'

Charlie stood up. 'Let's spread them out on the table. I've got the others over there too, in that blue folder.'

He slid out the pictures that he'd taken from the roof garden and arranged them carefully, to make a circular panorama. Mr Feinstein nodded approvingly.

'Not bad. But I thought you didn't believe in arranging photographs.'

'I don't believe in *inventing* arrangements,' Charlie said. 'This is different. I know just how these ought to go.'

He opened the blue file and took out the other pictures. Except one.

'They go right the way round,' he said, beginning to lay them out. 'With a line linking each detail to its proper part of the panorama.'

It was all there. The whole four miles of river, surrounded by the complex details of its plants and trees and water, in every season. Rich with all kinds of life, from the tiny waterboatmen skimming over the surface to the tall, stooped heron in the reeds.

Mr Feinstein stepped back, looking at the array of pictures. 'I like it! Will you put it up on the display board?'

'I don't mind,' Charlie said, trying not to grin. 'I'll get Jennifer to give me a hand. She's wonderful at things like that.'

He took the last picture out of the blue folder and laid it in the centre of the panorama, so that it was surrounded by the great loop of the river.

Mr Feinstein raised his eyebrows. 'I didn't know there were otters round here.'

'It's wonderful what you see,' Charlie said. 'If you know how to look.'

He stared down at the picture, gazing into the otter's remote, wild eyes. *They are elusive and nocturnal animals . . .*

He would never see it again. But, because he had seen it, he would look at the whole world in a different way. Wherever he turned, whenever he lifted his camera, there would be something new and beautiful.

And maybe, some day, he would see another otter, swimming free and strange in the bright river.